Also by Kelly J. Baptist

Isaiah Dunn Is My Hero

The Swag Is in the Socks

ISAIAH DUNN SAVES THE DAY

KELLY J. BAPTIST

CROWN BOOKS FOR YOUNG READERS

New York

Text copyright © 2022 by Kelly J. Baptist
Jacket art and interior illustrations copyright © 2022 by Adriana Bellet

Visit us on the Web! rhcbooks.com

Educators and librarians, for a variety of teaching tools, visit us at
RHTeachersLibrarians.com

Library of Congress Cataloging-in-Publication Data
Names: Baptist, Kelly J., author.
Title: Isaiah Dunn saves the day / Kelly J. Baptist.
Description: First edition. | New York: Crown Books for Young Readers, [2022] | Audience: Ages 8–12. | Audience: Grades 4–6. | Summary: Now in middle school, Isaiah Dunn participates in a mentoring program, but he has a hunch that his mentee—a troublemaking third-grader name Kobe—has a secret and Isaiah is determined to get to the bottom of it.
Identifiers: LCCN 2021057532 (print) | LCCN 2021057533 (ebook) | ISBN 978-0-593-42921-1 (hardcover) | ISBN 978-0-593-42922-8 (library binding) | ISBN 978-0-593-42923-5 (ebook)
Subjects: CYAC: Mentoring—Fiction. | Behavior—Fiction. | Poetry—Fiction. | African Americans—Fiction. | Middle schools—Fiction. | Schools—Fiction. | LCGFT: Novels.
Classification: LCC PZ7.1.B3674 It 2022 (print) | LCC PZ7.1.B3674 (ebook) | DDC [Fic]—dc23

The text of this book is set in 11-point Adobe Text Pro.
Interior design by Cathy Bobak

Printed in the United States of America
10 9 8 7 6 5 4 3 2 1
First Edition

Random House Children's Books supports the First Amendment
and celebrates the right to read.

For all the real-life Isaiahs: Keep being heroes!
And for Kobe, who will forever be mine.

August 18

" 'Saiah? 'Saiah, are you awake?"

I'm thinking maybe if I keep my eyes shut and breathe nice and slow, Charlie will get the hint and stop whisper-screaming in my ear.

Nope! Doesn't work! This is one of those times when I wonder why I ever asked for a little sister.

" 'Saiah!"

I groan and pull my blanket over my head.

"Char-lieee! I'm sleeping!"

"No, you're not; I see your eyes!" Charlie giggles, her little hands yanking my blanket back down. "Isaiah, guess what!"

"What?" I finally say with a sigh.

"There's only five days till my birthday! Five days till I'm five!"

Mama always says that Charlie's too smart for her own good, and now that Charlie's obsessed with the number five, I see what Mama means.

"Wow, Charlie, real nice," I say, turning over.

"'Saiah, you have to help me plan the party!" Charlie continues, tapping me on the back. "I want princesses and mermaids and Elmo."

Really, Charlie?

"Mama will help you plan," I tell her.

"But I want YOU!"

"I'll do it later," I mumble.

"Promise?" Charlie asks.

"Yeah."

"When you wake up?"

"YEAH!"

"Okay. But I thought Sneaky said to meet him at nine o'clock," Charlie says in this know-it-all voice. She's got this annoying habit of spying on me and my best friend, Sneaky.

I sit up quick and check my watch. 8:51.

"See, you're up! Now we can—"

"Later, Charlie!" I say, gently pushing her toward the door. She pouts, but she'll be okay.

I make my bed up fast and throw on shorts and a T-shirt.

"See ya later, Inka," I say to the mannequin in the room. For the past few months, me, Mama, and Charlie have been living with Miz Rita, who's like a grandma to us. The room I'm staying

in is Miz Rita's sewing room. I was scared of the sewing mannequin at first, but once I named her Inka, she stopped bothering
me. I even wrote a few stories about her, like *Inka, The Secret
Keeper.* To stop Charlie from being scared of the mannequin, I
told her that Inka would keep any secret she has. Now Charlie's
always busting in my room to whisper to Inka.

"Morning, Miz Rita," I say, popping into the kitchen. One
good thing about Miz Rita is that she *always* makes breakfast—
really good breakfast. Today it's biscuits, so I grab one to go.

"Morning, Isaiah. Where you off to so early?" Miz Rita asks.

"Gotta meet Sneaky at the playground," I say, smearing
grape jelly on my biscuit.

"You and Sneaky, huh?" Miz Rita chuckles. "Y'all make sure
you stay out of trouble."

"Miz Rita, we don't get in trouble," I say. It's kinda true, I
guess. You never know with Sneaky. He has a new business idea
he wants to start today, and Sneaky don't play when it comes to
his businesses and his money.

"Is Mama here?" I ask.

"She had some errands to run," Miz Rita says.

Mama's been running a lot of errands lately, but I know it's
probably because she's getting back on her feet. Pretty soon,
we're gonna have our own place again and things will be much
better.

"Oh snap, I gotta go!" I say, looking at my watch. I grab a
second biscuit and rush to the front door.

"I wanna come, too!" Charlie calls, trying to follow me.

"Not now, Charlie," I say over my shoulder. As I close the door behind me, I hear Miz Rita saying some nice stuff to keep Charlie from crying. I kinda feel bad, but I'll just read her a poem later.

"You late, bro," Sneaky says when I get to the playground.

"My bad," I say, even though it's only a few minutes after nine. Like I said, Sneaky don't play. He's standing by a bench and has a couple of small coolers sitting on it. He launches right into his idea.

"Yo, so it's too hot for candy, right? Check it out!"

Sneaky opens one of the coolers and there's a rainbow of colors inside. Freeze pops.

"The other one has water bottles. Perfect for a hot day, right?"

"I guess," I say. "But won't they melt?"

"Yeah, eventually," Sneaky says. "I put some ice in here, but we gotta sell them fast."

Sneaky's plan is to hit up all the playgrounds and parks that we can walk to—all the basketball courts, too.

"People be hot and thirsty and don't feel like going all the way home, so that's where we come in," he explains.

"Nice," I say. I grab one of the coolers and Sneaky grabs the other. We start at the playground by our building and sell eleven freeze pops in only a few minutes!

Sneaky pockets the dollars with a grin as we head to the basketball court around the block. At school, Sneaky's the candy man; since they took out all the vending machines, kids got real desperate for Snickers, gummy worms, and everything else. I guess for the last few weeks of summer, he's gonna be known as the freeze-pop man.

I don't mind being Sneaky's sidekick, but I got my own hustle, too. I'm a writer like my dad was, only he wrote stories and I do poems. Me and my friend Angel have a poetry business called @Dunn Poems. I come up with the poems, and she writes them real nice and pretty. Our business is on hold right now, though, cuz Angel's in Georgia for the whole summer! No offense to Sneaky, but she needs to hurry up and come home so *my* business can be back in business.

August 19

Miz Rita's apartment is aight, but my favorite place to be is the library. I used to sit in the same spot in the children's section, right by a window. That's where I would read Daddy's gold notebook and do my homework while I waited for Mama to pick me up. Now I head straight for my brand-new spot, the Gary Dunn Writing Room.

The room is named after my dad, and it was my idea to create it in this storage room that used to be full of junk. Mr. Shephard, the coolest librarian ever, helped me get permission from all the important library people, and then lots of companies donated furniture and computers for the room. It's nice and cozy, and my dad's words are on the walls. I always come up with good poems whenever I'm in the GD room.

"Isaiah, what's up, my man?" Mr. Shephard holds out a fist and I bump it with mine.

"Nothin' much, Mr. S," I say. "How's the room?"

"Perfect as always," Mr. Shephard says. "Pretty sure your spot's open."

"Cool," I say. "See you around."

"Hey, don't forget the summer reading program," Mr. Shephard reminds me. "Haven't stamped your board in a while."

"I gotcha, Mr. S," I say. I tell him he can get that stamp ready cuz I'm almost done with *The Crossover*.

Mr. Shephard salutes me and continues shelving books.

Two other people are in the GD room when I walk in, but Mr. Shephard was right; my spot's open. I always sit in a green beanbag in the corner. Daddy's words are in a picture frame right above the beanbag: *"A head held high means you see everything you're supposed to!"*

I drop my book bag on the floor and plop onto the beanbag. I always do the same thing when I come in here: read a few pages from Daddy's notebook and then start writing a poem. I always trip out when I see the title of Daddy's stories, *The Beans and Rice Chronicles of Isaiah Dunn*. When he was alive, Daddy wrote stories about a kid superhero named Isaiah Dunn, who got his powers from bowls of beans and rice. In the stories, Isaiah Dunn is always going on secret missions, solving mysteries, and saving everybody. In real life, beans and rice definitely don't give me powers. I've eaten enough bowls this year to last me for forever!

After I read about superhero Isaiah stopping a fight, I get out my own gold notebook and pen and start writing.

> why fight?
> Just be a friend.
> That's a battle
> That everyone wins.

I write a poem about how hot it is in the summer and one about library smells. The man sitting at one of the computer stations is typing away, and the kid in one of the yellow beanbags is reading a real big book. It's quiet in here, but all our words are saying a lot.

Daddy would really love this room.

What he would *not* love is the kid who comes into the GD room all loud, kicking one of the beanbags and complaining, "Don't nobody even wanna be here for the stupid story time!"

"Story time's out there, buddy," says the guy at the computer.

The kid, who has braids and is *super* short, sucks his teeth and glares at the guy. He picks a few books but doesn't open them, just tosses them on the shelf—and NOT neatly. After mumbling something about hating the library, the kid finally stomps off and the room is peaceful again.

On my way out, I fix the books that the kid left. When I find Mr. Shephard, we gotta talk about who's allowed in the GD room and who should stay a million miles away.

August 22

"You ever think about cutting hair, Isaiah?"

I'm at New Growth, the barbershop owned by my guy Rock, and his question makes me laugh.

"Nah," I say. "That's for you, not me."

"You never know," Rock says. It's Tuesday, which means the shop is slow, and Rock gets all deep and talkative. "People always need their hair cut; it's a nice little hustle."

"I already got a hustle, remember?" I hold up my notebook and pen.

"Yeah, you right," Rock says. "Just was thinking that we spend all this time together, might as well show you a few things."

"A few things like what?"

"Like what to do with these!" Rock says, holding up a pair of his clippers. When I think about it, Rock's clippers are like his beans and rice; they give him superpowers! Rock laughs when I tell him that.

"I guess you right, man," he says. "I definitely had to use my powers on that last guy; his hairline was no joke!"

"I'm gonna write a poem about how you hooked him up," I say, thinking about the man's hair. He came in with a short Afro that was flat on one side, and his hairline *was* pretty far back. When he left, his hair was all even and his edge-up was crispy.

> This barber's a hero
> With clippers in his hand.
> A comb in the other,
> And he's ready to jam!
> Your hair might be bad
> When you step in the shop,
> But just put on the cape
> And get ready to ROCK!

"You got a real gift, li'l man," Rock tells me. "Once you figure out what to do with it, you gonna do great things."

"I already know what I'm doing," I say. "@Dunn Poems."

Rock grins like he's got a secret.

"That's only scratching the surface, 'Saiah," he tells me. "Tip of the iceberg!"

Rock gets another customer so I don't get to ask him exactly what he means about the poem stuff. I stay busy sweeping up the hair after each person and making sure everything stays neat and tidy. I normally work at the shop on Tuesdays and Thursdays after school, but since it's summer, Rock said I can come by any day, even if it's just to chill or write.

Once things slow down a little, Rock shows me how to clean the clippers.

"I think this is gonna be one of your jobs, too, li'l man," he says, "once you get the hang of it. Safety's important, you know."

I nod, making sure I'm careful as I spray the pair of clippers Rock hands me. I wipe down the sides and brush all the hair from the blades.

"Good," Rock says. He checks his watch. "Alright, enough work, Isaiah. Time to enjoy all the sunshine out there."

I'm putting my notebook and pen in my backpack when Rock snaps his fingers.

"Almost forgot! Stay right there, I got something for you, li'l man."

Rock goes to the back where his office is and comes out a few minutes later with a bike.

"This is for you," he says, wheeling the bike over. "Nothing like exploring the city in the summer!"

The bike is black and gold like my notebook, and it has gold pegs so Sneaky can ride on the back. It still has the store tag on it, so I know it's brand new.

"This is for me? For real?"

"Yeah, for real!" Rock laughs. "Now you can ride to work in style."

"Thanks!" I say. I'm real excited about the bike, but it also makes me think about my last bike, the one Daddy gave me when I turned nine. I know I'm too big for it now, but I wonder if it's still in storage with the rest of our stuff.

Rock cuts off the tag and hands me a shiny black Mohawk helmet. "Here you go; let's see what it do!"

I get on the bike right there in the shop and push off. Rock swats my arm.

"Out *there*, li'l man!" he says. He opens the barbershop door, and I ride out onto the sidewalk.

It's hot, but I don't really mind. I ride down to the corner and come back. Rock's standing outside the barbershop, grinning just like my dad was when I rode the bike he got me. I swallow hard and grin back to make sure I stay sunny.

"There you go, Isaiah!" Rock calls. "It's a smooth ride, ain't it?"

"Yeah," I say. When I stop in front of the shop, I notice Rock's eyes shift to the right and he frowns a little.

"Ain't that your homeboy's brother?"

I turn to watch what Rock sees coming down the street. It's Sneaky's brother, Antwan, and two other guys.

"Yeah, that's Antwan," I say.

Rock shakes his head and sighs. "That boy needs to turn it around—quick."

I know exactly what Rock means. Antwan's fifteen, but he acts like he's grown already. I don't know what happened when he started high school, but he's a whole different person from two years ago.

"Yo, w'sup, 'Saiah," Antwan says, nodding toward me.

"Hey, Antwan," I say.

"Nice wheels," Antwan says, looking at my bike.

"Thanks," I say. "Rock gave it to me."

Antwan nods at Rock, too, but doesn't say anything.

"Looks like you could use a cut, youngblood," Rock says.

"Nah, I'm good," Antwan says.

"Aight, well, I'm here when you ready," Rock tells him.

"Yeah, aight," Antwan says. His friends tell him they gotta go, and they all keep walking. Both me and Rock watch him, and I'm hoping he'll turn around and come back, hang out in the shop, and let Rock cut his hair.

He doesn't.

August 23

"Wake up, 'Saiah! Wake up! It's my birthday! I'm five! I'm five! I'm five!"

Charlie's annoying, high-pitched voice rips me from a dream about Wakanda, and I have to blink a few times to remind myself I'm here at Miz Rita's and not off somewhere saving the world.

"Happy birthday," I tell her. She leans in, and I give her a quick hug before she starts bouncing up and down.

"You gotta get up and come to my special breakfast!" she says.

"I'm coming," I say. No use trying to go back to sleep. Charlie's way too amped, and she'll be singing "Happy Birthday" to herself all day long.

Whoa. My mouth drops open when I walk into the kitchen. Mama and Miz Rita are letting Charlie go way out for her birthday! For one, Charlie's wearing this pink princess dress with sparkles all over it, a pink crown, and pink Cinderella slippers, and she's waving around a pink wand that has the number five on it. For two, the kitchen looks like the color pink got sick and threw up everywhere. Balloons, streamers, and, like, a hundred fives hang from the ceiling. The table is set like a tea party, with blueberry pancakes, French fries, eggs, and applesauce on each plate and strawberry milk in the teacups. Charlie really got everything she's been talking about!

"Sit next to me, 'Saiah," Charlie says, pulling me to a chair.

I sit down and see that Charlie got a place set for Shayna, Miz Rita's granddaughter, even though she went to college last week. I don't have to ask who the other empty seat is for.

Mama and Miz Rita sit down, and Charlie says grace.

"Thank you, Jesus, for my birthday breakfast and my balloons and my magic wand and my princess dress, and for Mama and Miz Rita and Shayna and Daddy, even though he's missing my birthday, and thank you for my big brother, Isaiah. Please make him write me a poem for my birthday. Amen!"

We dig into the food, and I'm grinning cuz Charlie has no idea that I already wrote her poem. Actually, I made her a card—the very first @Dunn Poems card. Angel still ain't back, so I had to draw all the flowers and stuff by myself. It was mad hard, and I wasted a bunch of paper cuz I kept messing up. I think Charlie will like it though, especially the five-dollar bill I taped inside.

"After we eat we're watching *Finding Dory,* right, Mama?" asks Charlie. Since it's her birthday, I don't fuss at her about the blueberries and syrup all over her mouth and face. Yuck! I just hand her a napkin.

"Yes, baby, you can watch that with Isaiah while I clean up in here," Mama says.

I sigh, but not too loud, since it's her birthday. Charlie watches *Finding Dory* a billion times a week already, and most of those times I've had to sit with her and watch it, too!

"How 'bout a different movie, Charlie?" I ask. I name some of the kiddie movies that are out right now. Charlie pauses like she's thinking about it. *C'mon, c'mon!*

"Nope! *Finding Dory*!" she says, slurping her strawberry milk. I hand her another napkin for the milk mustache.

"C'mon, Isaiah, start the movie!" Charlie jumps up from her chair and races to the living room. Now I groan out loud. Miz Rita pats my arm.

"Like I always say, she's lucky to have a big brother like you," she says.

I take my plate and Charlie's to the sink, then go sit next to her on the couch and try not to fall asleep. I have my notebook with me, just in case all this underwater stuff makes me think of a poem.

By the time the movie's done, Mama's ready to go to the next part of Charlie's birthday celebration. We pack food and coolers in Miz Rita's car and climb in. Sneaky comes down to ride with us, too, since he doesn't want to wait for his mom and Wes, who's her boyfriend, to get off work.

Charlie's birthday party is gonna be at McReynolds Park, and even though Charlie really don't have a lot of friends, Mama still rented this giant princess bouncy house. She said with all the kids that be at the park, Charlie will be sure to make some friends.

Mama's right.

Tons of kids come running over to the bouncy house as soon as it's up, and they're all laughing and screaming in seconds. Me and Sneaky help Mama and Miz Rita hang up streamers in the picnic area. There's a banner that says, "The Princess Is Turning 5!!" and Sneaky looks at it and says, "Dang, they doing all this for five?"

"I know, right?" I say. My birthday was in June, and I definitely didn't get all this. I think maybe Mama feels guilty since she wasn't there for mine. Plus, Charlie's having so much fun, she won't focus on the fact that Daddy's missing.

After we help with all the princessy stuff, Sneaky and I play catch and walk around. McReynolds Park is pretty big, with picnic areas, bike trails, a lake, courts, and playground stuff. We always called it Bark Park, cuz we could never come here without hearing dogs barking up a storm. We see plenty of dogs on our walk, and Sneaky tosses me a pack of M&M's.

"That's, like, three," I say, popping the pieces in my mouth. We play this game where we eat a piece of candy each time we hear a dog bark. Sneaky made it up after Daddy died. When we would come with him, Daddy would promise to give us a dollar if we made it through the time without hearing a dog. Of course we'd hear tons of barking, but Daddy would still give us a dollar anyway.

"I saw Antwan yesterday," I say to Sneaky.

"So? Bet he was skipping summer school, right?"

"I guess." I shrug.

"Dumb," Sneaky says. "All they gonna do is call my mom, and then they'll be getting into it."

"Maybe he went to school today," I say, even though we both know he probably didn't. We keep walking until we finish the last of the M&M's.

"I'm starving!" Sneaky says.

"They probably got the food ready by now," I tell him. We been walking for a while, and we're both ready to head back.

16

Mama races up to me as soon as we get to the picnic area. Sneaky's mom and Wes are right behind her. None of their faces look normal. My stomach starts doing this karate-chop thing that only happens when I'm nervous. Or when something is wrong.

"'Saiah, did Charlie go with you?" Mama asks.

"No, she was in the bouncy house," I say. My heart beats faster as Mama's eyes dart all around.

"She's probably still in there, Miz Lisa," Sneaky says. "I'ma go check!"

"I'm going to check the playground, Lisa," Wes says.

"I'm going down by the lake," Sneaky's mom says. "Miz Rita's gonna stay in this area in case she comes back."

Everyone takes off, but I'm frozen. I know Charlie likes to follow me around, but what if she tried to now and got lost? I squeeze my eyes shut and try to imagine where she'd go. She loves the swings, and she loves to run around. I thought she'd love the bouncy house, too! I wish I had a magic bowl of beans and rice to give me a Charlie-locator superpower.

I don't have to wonder about it for long because a few minutes later, Wes comes back and he's holding Charlie's hand. A small part of me is thinking *I* should've found her, not Wes.

"Charlie, where were you?" demands Mama after hugging her close.

Charlie holds up a kite and grins.

"Look! My new friend gave me a kite! She's over there; can she have some of my birthday cake?"

Mama scolds Charlie about wandering off.

"You had everybody really worried about you," Mama says.

"Sorry, Mama," Charlie says in a small voice. "I just wanted to see the pretty kite."

Charlie moves closer to me, and I put my arm around her. I can tell she's about to cry, which really sucks. You shouldn't have to cry on your birthday! I bet I can do something about that!

"Hey, Charlie, you just gotta tell us next time, okay?" I say. She nods, but tears still splash her cheeks.

"Check it out, I got something for you," I say, pulling off my book bag and unzipping it. I reach inside and grab the birthday card I made for Charlie. She wipes her eyes and opens the card.

> I don't need more,
> I don't need less.
> Got 1 li'l sis,
> And she's the
> BEST!!

"Oooh, pink butteyflies!" Charlie says, her smile coming back. "You writed this, 'Saiah?"

"Yeah, I *wrote* it," I say. The poem is really simple so Charlie can read it herself. I think she likes the words more than the money! When she's done, she gives me a huge hug and asks me to help her fly the kite.

I'm super hungry, and I can smell the hot dogs that Wes is grilling, but I help Charlie with the kite. When it's time to eat, I fix her the perfect birthday plate. I'm probably the only one who knows she likes ketchup, mayo, and crunched-up potato chips on her hot dogs, and she has to put her cake on *top* of her ice cream.

By the time we get back home, I'm exhausted! Being a hero big brother is hard work, but it's up to me to do it!

August 25

"I have a big announcement to make," Mama says while we're eating the turkey burgers Miz Rita made for dinner.

FINALLY!!! Mama's been looking for apartments, and I bet she finally found one! We used to live in this same building, on the seventh floor, so my fingers are crossed that a place opened up here.

"What is it, Mama?" Charlie asks. She's got mayo smeared on her cheek. Yuck! "Are we getting a dog?"

"No." Mama laughs. "Not a dog, Charlie baby."

"Yeah, Charlie, that would mean more messes to clean up!" I add.

"I don't make messes!" Charlie says, dropping a French fry in her lap. I laugh.

"Okay, do y'all wanna hear the news or not?" Mama asks.

"YES!" me and Charlie say at the same time.

Miz Rita doesn't say anything cuz she probably already knows. Her and Mama always be talking in the kitchen, sipping tea or coffee. Mama calls it their "mug sessions."

"Well, in a few weeks, when Isaiah starts middle school and my Charlie baby starts kindergarten, Mama will be going to school, too!"

Huh?

"But, Mama, you're too big to go to school with me and Isaiah!" Charlie says. Her face is all scrunched up like she can't figure out what's going on.

"No, baby," laughs Mama, "I won't be going to your or Isaiah's school. I'll be going to my own school."

"They make school for big people?" asks Charlie.

"Yeah, Charlie, it's called college, remember?" I say. "You mean college, right, Mama? Like where Shayna is?"

Mama takes a bite of her burger and nods.

"I thought you did college already," I say. Now *my* face is scrunched up like Charlie's.

"I did," Mama says. "But this is a little different. It's like an extra year after college."

"For what?" I ask. I don't know why anyone would want *more* school!

"Well, it will help me learn more about something I'm interested in," Mama says. "And you know what else? I also got a job on campus."

I don't ask any more questions, not even the ones that keep floating around in my brain: *Is Mama gonna wait a whole year before we move? Are we gonna live with Miz Rita forever?*

Don't get me wrong; Miz Rita's cool and all. But it's still kinda weird to live in somebody else's house, especially someone who only buys healthy juice—no pop, *ever*—watches shows like *Family Feud, The Price Is Right,* and *Jeopardy!,* and says the lights go off in her house at 10 p.m., even on summer break! Miz Rita told us we can stay as long as we need to, but I didn't think Mama would have us here forever! I'm happy about her school and all, but I'm starting to get a worried feeling in my stomach.

"You alright, Isaiah?" Mama asks me in the kitchen later. It's not my night to wash dishes, but I do it anyway, to help out.

"Yeah," I say, scrubbing a plate.

"Mmmhmmm," Mama says. "I know you probably worryin' about everything, but all you need to do the rest of the summer is have fun. Run around with Sneaky, hang out at the library. I got this."

I don't say anything. Mama really hasn't "got this" since Daddy died, and I'm hoping real hard that things are changing.

"You not talking now, but I bet you gonna go write a poem about this, aren't you!" Mama says, nudging me.

"I think I'm just gonna read tonight," I say. Mama nods and rubs my shoulder. She must have some superpowers in her fingers, cuz I start to feel a little better . . . better enough to write a poem before I go to sleep.

August 26

"Got some news for you, li'l man," Rock tells me as soon as I wheel my bike into the shop.

"What happened?" I ask. He has a big smile on his face so I know it's gotta be good.

"Check it out!" Rock hands me a letter, and the first thing I see is *Eugene Rockman, New Growth Barbershop,* which makes me crack up.

"Your name is Eugene?" I say with a laugh.

Rock swats my arm. "Boy, stop clowning my name and read the whole thing!"

When I see the next word—*Congratulations!*—I get excited, cuz it reminds me of when I read the email that said Daddy's story won second place in the library's short-story contest. I keep reading to find out what Rock entered.

"What's the First Cut Competition?" I ask.

"It's an annual thing where the best barbers in the country battle it out for the title of King or Queen of the Clippers," Rock tells me. I read the letter again. Yooo, First Cut is inviting Rock to compete!

"Yeeaaaah, Rock!" I say, holding out my fist. He daps me up, then says something I don't expect.

"You know I have you to thank for this, Isaiah," he says.

"Me? Why you say that?"

"You inspired me," Rock explains. "I keep thinking about what you did for your dad, and how you stay on your grind. I get information on this competition every year, and I always pass. This year, I said, let me go ahead and enter. So I did."

"And they picked you," I say with a grin.

"They picked me!" Rock laughs. "I'm gonna be like you when I grow up!"

"You already grown, Rock," I say, shaking my head. He always says wild stuff like that.

"Yeah, I am, but that don't mean I can't be inspired by a young person like you," Rock tells me. "As long as you're alive, there's always growing to do, li'l man."

I guess he has a point. You can always get better at what you do. I grab the broom and sweep while Rock tells me what will happen next.

"I'll be closing the shop for a few days next week," he says. "First time I ever did that."

"You feel nervous?" I ask.

"Nervous?" Rock strokes his beard and thinks for a second. "There might be a few butterflies, li'l man, but mostly it's excitement. I get to show the world my skills."

I always hear people talk about having butterflies in their stomach, but for me, it's a little different. Me and Daddy used to watch old kung fu movies together, and when I get nervous it feels like somebody's karate-chopping in my stomach!

Rock starts getting customers so I get busy with sweeping, cleaning the clippers, and wiping down the chair between people. I also spray all the mirrors and windows with Windex and make sure they're sparkling clean.

"Man, I wish I could take you with me to Atlanta!" Rock jokes once the barbershop is empty again.

"Me too," I say. Atlanta is where Angel is. She hasn't emailed me like she said she would so I guess she's having too much fun. Sneaky's right; @Dunn Poems shouldn't be on pause just because she's gone.

I take a break and open my notebook to jot down ideas. Words start flowing right away, which is completely different from a few months ago. When me, Mama, and Charlie lived in the Smoky Inn, my words wouldn't come out at all. I'm glad they do now!

words don't wait,
so why should I?
Move ahead,
No time to cry.
words won't wait,
so let them come.
Keeping them in
Just isn't fun.
Ideas come

And ideas go.
when you feel the words,
Just let them flow.

The door to the barbershop dings, and Mrs. Rock (that's what I call her) comes in with a few boxes of doughnuts and some balloons.

"Hey, Isaiah, how you doing?" she asks.

"I'm good," I say. "How 'bout you?"

"I'm fabulous," she says. "Did Rock tell you the news?"

"Yep," I say, and I can't hide the grin on my face. "Y'all are going to Atlanta!"

"Indeed we are!" she says. "I thought the shop could use some celebration vibes."

I help her arrange the doughnuts, balloons, and napkins on a small table, and when Rock comes back up front, he's got a real surprised look on his face.

"What's all this?"

"It's excitement, baby," Mrs. Rock says, giving him a big hug.

It's a busy Saturday and people congratulate Rock the rest of the afternoon. I eat three doughnuts, keep the shop spotless, and every time I have a free second, I let my words flow.

August 28

"Can't believe they makin' us come to this!" Sneaky groans as we walk into the packed middle-school lobby for this orientation thing. He's complaining that his mom wouldn't let him bring candy to sell, but I'm busy looking for Angel. I don't see her anywhere! Man, when is she coming back?

"At least they got food," Sneaky says. We split from our moms and head over to where our friends Gabi, Jules, Mike O, and Aliya are grabbing snacks off a table.

"Yo, I'm gonna call you Shorty instead of Sneaky!" Mike O says with a laugh. Him and Jules got mad tall over the summer, and it feels like me and Sneaky haven't grown at all.

"Man, shut up!" Sneaky punches Mike O's shoulder.

"I want a Snickers," Aliya announces. "You got candy, Shorty?"

"Nah, you stuck with this!" Sneaky tosses some popcorn at Aliya. She squeals and tosses some back.

"Awww, look at the lovebirds!" says Jules, recording them on his phone. Everybody knows Sneaky and Aliya like each other, even if they won't admit it.

"Isaiah, where's *your* girlfriend?" teases Mike O. I fling some popcorn his way.

We're still laughing and joking when an announcement comes over the loudspeaker that everyone needs to move into the auditorium for the program.

"Time to be bored!" groans Sneaky as we follow the crowd of people inside. We all sit together in the back and try not to laugh too loud while the principal and other people talk about the school and rules and blah blah blah. When all the talking's finally done, they tell us to go to the gym to get our schedules and locker assignments.

The gym is set up with tables, and I guess we're supposed to go around and sign up for clubs and stuff. Mike O beelines for the sports table, and the girls wander over to a table with those pom-pom things on it. Me, Sneaky, and Jules go to check out the robotics table, but someone calls my name before I make it over there.

"Hey, Isaiah!"

I look over and see Ms. Marlee waving at me. She's at a table with a huge banner that says ROCKET RESTORE. In fifth grade, Ms. Marlee was the lady you went to if you got in trouble and had to talk to somebody. When me and Angel had our fight, we had to do the Rocket ReStore program with Ms. Marlee. I guess you could say it worked, cuz we definitely don't fight anymore.

"Hey, Ms. Marlee," I say.

"I was hoping you'd be here," Ms. Marlee says. "Do you have a second?"

"Um, I guess so," I say, watching Jules and Sneaky at the robotics table.

"I won't take long," Ms. Marlee says. "You already know

about Rocket ReStore, but I wanted to tell you about Rockets Reach Back. It's a mentorship program where students at the middle school are matched with a student at the elementary school. We meet once a week and talk about things like bullying, doing well in school, making friends, and more. Who knows, we might do some writing as well!"

Ms. Marlee hands me a brochure and winks. "I think you'd be really good with this, Isaiah, so if you're interested, just fill out the back part of that brochure and get it to me anytime, okay?"

"Okay," I say. I fold the brochure and stick it in my pocket, then hurry to catch up with Sneaky. When I get to the robotics table, Sneaky's asking the people there if the middle school has a money club. Jules snickers.

"A money club?" asks the lady.

"Yeah, for people who are all about that money!" Sneaky says. The man and lady look at each other like, what is this kid talking about? They suggest some clubs to Sneaky and move us along, but Sneaky's already talking about how he's gonna start his own club.

I forget all about the brochure from Ms. Marlee until I'm back in my room at Miz Rita's. I unfold it and see pictures of smiling kids everywhere. Charlie's enough to deal with already and Ms. Marlee thinks I should work with more little kids? No thanks! I toss the brochure over by Inka and grab one of Daddy's notebooks from my green basket. Maybe he wrote something about starting middle school and how to pick the right club. I know the notebooks are just words, but anything from Daddy really helps.

August 31

Sneaky's business is on pause since we sold out of everything. He's been begging his aunt to take him to FoodMax, where he can buy a whole lot of freeze pops, but no luck yet. I don't mind too much, cuz now I get to sleep in a little and work on @Dunn Poems. Also means I get to go to the library without Sneaky clowning me about it.

The writing room is empty today, so I get on a computer and start typing up some of my poems. I check my email, and my mouth drops open when I see a message from Angel! When I start reading, it's just like with Daddy's stories; I can hear Angel's voice in my head.

> What's up, Isaiah, how's your summer going? Mine is HOT! My granny don't have no AC and that is NOT a good look. We down here melting! Guess what? I got an idea that's gonna take our business to the next level. . . . Greeting cards! It hit me last night at my

granny's birthday dinner. People are always buying cards, you know? So we should sell them! Anyway, gotta go! I'll send you a list of all the things we need next time I go to the library. That's where I'm at right now, cuz my granny also don't have Wi-Fi! I bet you're at the library right now, too, aren't you? ☺ Have fun and write lots of poems!
~Angel

PS: I don't know when I'm comin' back. My parents keep saying they love it down here. Crazy, right?

I read Angel's email two more times. It's all good until the end. For the first time I think, *What if Angel doesn't come back?* I only write one poem, and it's short.

Moving around is great,
unless you need to stay.
Atlanta doesn't need you anyway . . .

Writing the word *Atlanta* makes me think about Rock's trip. He flew down there today, but he'll be back on Tuesday. Angel should be more like him; go down there for a little while and come right back.

I type in "Atlanta First Cut Competition" and see all this stuff with barbers cutting hair and winning in different categories. Tomorrow is Day 1 of the competition. I look through all the pictures, but I don't see him. I do see his name, though: Eugene Rockman. I crack up again. Eugene!

I log off the computer, grab my book bag, and leave the writing room. In the children's section, Mr. Shephard is doing story time, reading to a group of kids who are paying attention to the book he's got in his hands . . . except for this one kid with braids. The same kid who was making a mess in the GD room when we were selling freeze pops!

"Man, this book SUCKS!" the kid says. He's not sitting still on the floor like everyone else, and the other kids are looking at him like, will somebody come get this dude?

"It's okay if you don't like the story," Mr. Shephard says, "but you need to sit quietly so the other kids can enjoy it, okay?"

The kid makes a face but doesn't answer. He doesn't sit still, either.

I shake my head as I leave. I don't know how Mr. Shephard does it. I think about Ms. Marlee and how she wants me to work with some bad little kids like that. I don't think so!

September 5

BAM!

It's the first day of school, and I'm eating breakfast with Sneaky in the cafeteria when a tray slams on the table right next to me. I jump and look up.

"Ready to get to work?"

Angel stands over me with a smirk on her face. I don't know whether to yell at her or give her a hug. Sneaky would definitely clown me on the hug thing, so I leave that one alone.

"Took you long enough!" I say. "I thought you weren't coming back!"

"I know, right?" Angel says. "My mama and daddy waited till the last second, literally!"

Angel starts telling me the story of how her family drove through the night from Atlanta to get home.

"I mean, they were down there looking at schools for us and everything!" Angel says.

Sneaky clears his throat loudly when Angel sits down.

"This is a jerk-free table, sooo . . . ," he says.

I punch his arm and whisper, "Chill!" but Angel just laughs.

"Whatever, Sneaky. If it's jerk-free, you should be moving, right?"

"Dang, I see you still can't take a joke," Sneaky says.

"And I see you still *are* a joke!" Angel claps back.

"What classes do you have?" I ask quickly, before Sneaky says something else.

"The normal boring stuff, plus art," Angel says, pouring milk over her Frosted Flakes. "I'm just glad we don't have to see Mrs. Fisher's face anymore!"

"Facts," I say. Mrs. Fisher wasn't a bad teacher; I just don't think she liked me. Hopefully all my middle-school teachers will.

Sneaky's got on new shoes, of course, and he keeps studying them.

"Relax, Sneaky, they're clean," I say.

"Yeah, and they better stay that way!" Sneaky says. "Don't worry; you gonna be in the game soon, 'Saiah."

He's right. I got enough money now to buy some expensive shoes like his, but I don't know. I'm saving for something bigger. . . . I just don't know what.

The bell rings and we head off to our advisory, which we all have together. Angel sits with some of her friends, and me and Sneaky sit in the back.

"Bro," Sneaky says. "I wouldn't trust her if I were you."

Sneaky's wrong about Angel, and I tell him that.

"She's cool, Sneaky. Remember how she told me about who stole my money? Even though it was her cousin?"

"And remember how that dude bought a game with your money? Who snatched that game from him?" Sneaky says.

"You both helped me," I tell him. "You're both my friends."

Sneaky shakes his head but doesn't say anything else. I don't, either. There's gotta be a way to make my two business partners like each other!

After school, I race to the barbershop, and when I see Rock's grin from the window, I instantly know.

"Li'l man!" Rock says, pausing from his haircut to lift his arms in the air.

"You won?"

"I'm the King of the Clippers!" Rock shouts.

"I knew it!" I say.

I hold out my fist so me and Rock can do the Barbershop Shake. Rock daps me, and then we slap hands three times and salute each other.

"Yo, I just had a feeling you were gonna win!" I tell him.

"Of course you did, superhero!" Rock says. "You know a whole lot about winning, don't you?"

"Yeah, I guess I do," I say, thinking about how Daddy's words won a contest and now they're in a room in the library. Daddy's words help me find mine, and I know exactly what I'm gonna write next!

WINNER

Whenever things are dark
And you feel like you might lose,
You have to keep on trying,
It's the best thing you could choose!
You'll find that you are stronger
Than you thought that you could be.
So instead of giving up,
Keep going for the victory!

"Check it out, Rock," I say, showing him the page in my notebook once he's done with cutting hair. "Whatchoo think?"

Rock reads my poem and his eyes do that tearing-up thing again.

"I think this needs to be hanging on the wall at my new shop!" Rock says.

"My friend Angel can write it real pretty," I tell him. Then I stop. "Wait, what did you say? A new shop?"

Rock grins.

"The missus and I talked about it the whole flight back," Rock says. "When I opened this barbershop, it was always my dream to have another one. My brother always said, 'You gotta have a Now dream and a Later dream.' He always liked those Now and Later candies, so maybe that had something to do with it."

"Now you can tell him you got your Later dream," I say.

Rock shakes his head. "Nah, li'l man, the second New Growth is my *Now* dream!" Rock says.

"Huh?" I ask. "Then what's your Later dream?"

"A barber school," Rock says. "I'm gonna open my own school and train the youngbloods to cut hair, maybe help them open their own shops."

"That's cool," I say. It seems like a really big dream, but knowing Rock, he'll make it happen.

I help Rock put a banner outside his door that says "King of the Clippers, First Cut Competition Winner." Rock stares at that sign with a huge smile on his face. Too bad he can't stand out there for long!

The shop stays busy; real busy for a Tuesday, Rock says. I

guess a lot of people heard about Rock winning the competition. Rock keeps telling everyone, "New Growth #2 is on the way, y'all!" and everyone is as excited as he is. I wonder where the new shop will be, and if I'll be able to get to it on my bike.

When Rock edges up this guy with locs, I get out my notebook and write *NOW DREAMS* and *LATER DREAMS*. Under *NOW*, I put the greeting card idea for @Dunn Poems. Under *LATER*, I put . . . nothing. I can't think of a big dream like Rock's. Buying us a humongous house and whatever toys Charlie wants? Getting a Ferrari when I'm older? That was Daddy's favorite car, and I used to tell him I was going to buy him one. The car's a good dream, but it's really not mine.

"It'll come to you, Isaiah," Rock says, handing his customer a mirror to check himself out. Yo, how did he even see my notebook page? Superhero eyes, I guess.

"Hope you're right," I mumble under my breath.

"I usually am," he says with a wink. Rock must have superhero ears, too! It's gotta be the clippers!

September 8

"Was it your dream to work in a library?" I ask Mr. Shephard. It seems like a weird dream to me, but hey, maybe Mr. S really liked books when he was a kid.

"Absolutely not!" Mr. Shephard says with a laugh. He and I are wiping down the computers in the GD room. I been thinking about Now and Later dreams all week. Mama and Miz Rita are probably tired of all my questions, so now it's Mr. Shephard's turn.

"I wanted to be a pilot," Mr. Shephard tells me. "Went into the Air Force right after high school, and that's when I got the shock of my life."

"What happened?" I ask.

"I found out I don't really like being up in the air!" Mr. Shephard says. "So I had a lot to adjust."

"And that's when you became a librarian," I say.

"Nope!" Mr. Shephard says. "I went to college for architecture."

"You were an architect?" I ask.

"Not quite," Mr. Shephard throws his wipe away and rearranges some of the books in the room. "In my second year of school I had this literature class, and we had an enormous amount of books that we had to read. I was going to libraries all over the city to find copies. On top of all that, I was a slow reader and I needed peace and quiet to concentrate."

"I'm like that, too!" I say. "My little sister, Charlie, makes so much noise! That's why I always come here."

"Sounds like a normal little sister," Mr. Shephard says.

"Trust me; Charlie ain't normal," I say, which makes Mr. S

chuckle. He says he's glad the library is a place I like to get away to and that it reminds him of how he was in college.

"You gotta finish your story, Mr. S," I tell him.

"It's pretty simple from here. I went to this one library so much, one day they asked me if I was interested in a part-time job." Mr. Shephard waves a book in the air. "Shelving these guys!"

"I could do that," I say. "Maybe I'll work at a library, too."

"Yep, I definitely fell in love with it," Mr. Shephard says. "Changed my plans *again,* and went to library school."

"My mom's going to school, too," I say.

"That's really cool, Isaiah. What's she going to study?"

I shrug, cuz I don't really know. I guess I've been so busy worrying about my business and middle school and Sneaky and Angel that I haven't even asked her what her school is about, or if she likes her work. It could be one of her Now and Laters!

"Well, I'm sure she's going to do great, just like her son," Mr. Shephard says. He heads back to the children's section and I stay to read until Mama picks me up.

"Mama, do you like your job?" I ask as we drive home. Mama chuckles.

"It's actually called an assistantship, and that's where you help a professor with different things, sometimes grading papers or looking things up," she says. "And yes, I like it. I like being around learning. Kinda like how you love being around books."

"I guess so," I say. "But just so you know, I'm not gonna do forever school like you, Mama."

Mama laughs the best laugh ever.

"'Saiah, I promise I won't make you do forever school," she says. "Only enough to help you become a world-famous writer!"

"Bet," I say.

When we get home, I grab Daddy's notebook and write real close to his words:

Mama's doing big things,
following her Now and Later dreams.
She's really just like you.
Since you're not here to see,
I'll make sure I do.

September 11 ✏️

It's never pretty when Angel gets mad, and maaannn, she is mad right now!

We're at lunch and this whole thing started when Angel asked if I'm going to some meeting for Rockets Reach Back after school. I told her no and kept munching on my nachos. If eyes could slice, Angel would have me in pieces right now!

"You're not doing Rockets Reach Back?" she asks, giving me a look. "Didn't Ms. Marlee talk to you about it?"

"Yeah, but I'm not doing it," I say.

"Why not?" Angel demands. I shrug.

Angel shakes her head.

"What?" I ask. It's not really a big deal; I don't know why she's trippin'!

"Yeah, he don't wanna do it; so what?" Sneaky says. Maaannn, that gets Angel riled up even more!

"Nobody asked you, Sneaky! Stick to candy!"

"Since you said that," Sneaky says, unzipping his lunch pack. "Snickers? M&M's? All for the low price of a dollar!"

Angel rolls her eyes and ignores Sneaky. She doesn't ignore me.

"Isaiah, Ms. Marlee is counting on us for the program," she argues.

"Ummm, no she's not," I say. "She probably has other kids."

"I think you should do it," Angel says. "Just think about how that will look for our business!"

"Huh?"

"We're gonna have a website and everything! Adults will be happy to support a business that gives back," Angel says. "We could get sponsors, investors, who knows!"

"Whoa, whoa, whoa!" Sneaky interrupts. "Since when did you become Miss Business Lady?"

"You not the only one who can make money, Sneaky," Angel says. Sneaky makes a face like he doesn't believe her. Lunch is gonna suck if the two of them keep going back and forth all the time! I'm about to tell them to chill out, but then Aliya comes and sits next to Sneaky. He's all grins after that!

Angel's not.

"For real, Isaiah. You better join Rockets Reach Back."

"I don't have that paper thing anymore," I tell her, even though I'm pretty sure it's still by Inka.

Angel sighs all extra loud and shakes her head. She opens her pink folder, pulls out a paper, and slides it to me.

"Here," she says, plopping down a pen on top of it. "I got an extra one when Ms. Marlee told me you didn't turn yours in yet."

Sneaky starts cracking up.

"Dang, she got you in check, huh?"

I suck my teeth.

"I'll think about it," I tell Angel, pushing the pen back toward her.

"Well, think fast," Angel says, tapping her fingers on the table. "Training starts tomorrow after school. Your mom can sign it later."

And just like that, she gets up and walks to another table.

"Yo, you should just throw that away," Sneaky says, watching me fold the Rockets Reach Back paper into a tiny square. "We're doing football anyway, right?"

Sneaky found out about the Junior Football League at that open house, and now he wants all of us to play on the sixth-grade team.

I shrug and stuff the square in my pocket. What if Angel's right, and being in Rockets Reach Back will help our business? Or what if it would be better for me to play football with Sneaky?

In my room later, I unfold the paper and stare at it.

"What you think I should do?" I ask Inka. Of course, she doesn't say anything. But when I tell Mama about it, she starts talking right away!

"You must mean this," she says, rummaging around in her bag and pulling out a Rockets Reach Back brochure.

"Where'd you get that?" I ask.

"It was in your laundry basket," Mama says. "Are you thinking about signing up?"

"Uhhhh . . ."

"I think it would be great," Mama tells me. She says she had a mentor when she did college the first time and that it helped her a lot.

"And remember when Shayna was telling us about her navigator?" Mama continues. I nod. Shayna said her navigator helped her move in, gave her a tour of the campus, and even had a gift bag for her.

"I think you should do it, Isaiah," Mama says. "You're already a fantabulous big brother, so I know you'll be good at this." She's already reaching for a pen to sign the paper. Makes me wonder if Angel called and talked to her.

I think of how Charlie looks up to me and wants to do everything I do. Maybe it wouldn't be so bad if another little kid looked up to me, too.

Mama hands me the pen and I write my name as fancy as I can. But instead of feeling as excited as Mama looks, why do I feel like I just signed my life away?

September 13

The middle-school library is really nice, probably because not a lot of kids come in here. It kinda reminds me of the GD room, only bigger. There are lots of computers in the lab and comfy chairs near windows, just how I like it. Only thing missing is Mr. Shephard.

"Alright, guys, take out your journals and write your response to what you just saw," Ms. Marlee says. We're at our second Rockets Reach Back training, and we just watched a video about kids at a school all going through something that no one else knew about. There was a kid who was homeless, and it made me think about the time me, Mama, and Charlie had to live in our car. No one at my school except Sneaky knew about that.

"Isaiah, can you share some of your thoughts about the video?" Ms. Marlee asks.

"Ummm, I wrote that sometimes kids aren't mad at a teacher," I say. "They might just be mad about something else."

"That's right," Ms. Marlee says. "Some of the students you'll work with will be upset about things that have nothing to do with school. It'll be important for you to be patient and hear the story they tell and the story they don't tell."

Huh?

"What you mean, Ms. Marlee?" Angel asks loudly.

"You already know, Angel!" Ms. Marlee. "Sometimes kids don't tell everything they're thinking about. That doesn't mean we give up on them."

"All this stuff seems hard," says this kid Jalen. A few other kids nod.

"That's one way to put it," Ms. Marlee says. "I prefer the word *opportunity*. We have the opportunity to help other humans discover some beautiful things about themselves."

"That do sound good," Angel says. "But I don't know if I'ma be able to do all that."

"You'll be surprised at what you can do, Angel," Ms. Marlee says. "What *all* of you can do."

I look around the room. There's seven of us, all wearing red and yellow Rockets Reach Back T-shirts. Ms. Marlee gave them to us on the first day, said they make us official. Other than Angel, the only other person I know is Tayshaun, the kid who did the Rocket ReStore thing with me and Angel after our fight. He's an eighth grader now, so he probably knows everything.

"In the next few weeks, each of you will be matched with an elementary school student. We'll all meet once a week after school, and we'll have a few field trips as well."

"See? That's cool, right?" Angel whispers, nudging my arm. I shrug. I'm still not a hundred percent sure about this, but I guess going on a field trip would be nice. Ms. Marlee talks about some other things we'll get to do, and I start to feel a little better.

After the meeting, Angel and I sit outside on the benches and do some business planning until our rides get here.

"Check this out," Angel says, showing me a sample card. I can't lie; it really looks amazing! It's a birthday poem I wrote, and Angel copied it on this thick paper called cardstock and drew birthday cakes and balloons all over it. I grin as I read my words in Angel's fancy writing:

I don't have any money,
this poem is all I've got.
I'm so broke it ain't even funny,
so I couldn't get you a lot.

Please accept this card because
I did the best I could.
If I had more dead presidents,
I would've gotten you something good!

"Do you have the Christmas poems?" Angel asks.

"No," I say, wrinkling my nose. "It's September!"

"Duh! We gotta have a sample card for the holidays *before* the holidays," Angel says, raising an eyebrow. "You serious about this or what?"

"Yeah," I say. I reach in my book bag for my notebook. "I'll write a Christmas poem right now!"

I'm working on my first line when Angel's ride pulls up. I think it's her dad. He rolls down the window and calls, "Let's go, Angel!"

"That your dad?" I ask.

"Yeah," Angel says, packing up her things.

"Is he mad?" I ask. I remember Angel telling me her parents argued a lot and her dad sometimes said some mean things.

"Nah, he's not mad!" Angel says. "He's been a whole lot better since he got hired." She pulls my arm. "You should come meet him!"

"Hold up," I say. But Angel's already trotting off toward the car, so there's nothing to do but follow her.

"This is my business partner, Isaiah," Angel says.

"So you're the Word Man," Angel's dad says. He holds out his fist and I dap it.

"Hi," I say.

"Keep up the good work," Angel's dad tells me. "Angel's always talkin' 'bout @Dunn Poems this and @Dunn Poems that. Since we gotta listen to all that, I hope that means I get a birthday card!"

"Yeah, we can do that," I say. "When's your birthday?"

"End of the month, so y'all betta get to it!" Angel's dad laughs as Angel climbs into the car.

"See ya," Angel says. "Make sure you get the holiday ones done!"

"I will," I say. "You make sure the artwork is tight!"

Angel gives me a look like *Puh-leaze!* and her dad pulls off just as Mama pulls in. When I climb in the car with her, I can't help thinking what it would be like if it was Daddy picking me up instead.

September 14

"So how's them Now 'n' Later dreams coming, li'l man?" asks Rock. I'm the last haircut of the day, and I'm glad Rock isn't too tired to get me in. His clippers buzz close to my ear, and I squeeze my eyes closed to stay perfectly still. Once, Sneaky jumped while he was getting his hair cut and ended up with a bald head. I'm not gonna make the same mistake!

"It's coming okay, I guess," I tell Rock. "I just don't have no big dreams like you."

"Maybe not yet," Rock says. "Or maybe you do, and you just don't know it."

Rock tells me him and Mrs. Rock have been looking at places for his next barbershop.

"We've seen a lot of places, but this building over in Oak-wood Plaza? It's the one. The minute we walked in, I felt it."

"So you're gonna get it?" I ask. My eyes are still closed, cuz Rock is lining up my other side.

"That's the plan," Rock says. "Can't wait for you to bless it."

"Bless it?"

"Yessir!" Rock says. He points to the opposite wall. I didn't notice when I came in, but Rock framed my poem and hung it up!

"Whoa!" I say. Rock chuckles and dusts me off.

It feels good to see my words in a frame. It's just like Daddy's words in the GD room. Words start filling my mind for Rock's next poem, and I grab my notebook.

"Make it good, now! I know exactly which—"

Rock stops mid-sentence and I turn so I can see him. He's watching something outside, and then lightning fast, he drops his clippers on the chair and rushes out, yelling at me to stay inside.

I drop my notebook and peek outside. There's a group of guys down the street and most of them scatter when Rock gets closer. Rock reaches down and pulls someone up. Then Rock's helping whoever it is walk toward the shop. My stomach starts karate-chopping when they get to the door and I see who's with Rock.

It's Antwan.

September 15

I don't remember falling asleep, but I guess I do cuz I wake up in the middle of the night to Charlie's knee in my back. I blink and turn over.

"Charlie! Charlie, what you doing in here?" I whisper. No answer. I'm about to shake her awake and send her back to her room when there's a flash and loud *BOOM!* outside. Charlie flinches in her sleep and scoots closer to me.

I used to be scared of thunderstorms, too—a long, long time ago, before Charlie was even born. I would climb into Mama and Daddy's bed, right in the middle, cuz then the thunder couldn't get me. In *The Beans and Rice Chronicles of Isaiah Dunn,* Daddy wrote about superhero Isaiah Dunn stopping a never-ending thunderstorm. When I read that story, I knew Daddy was writing about me.

I lay back down and listen to the rain outside. I guess it *is* kinda scary when the lightning flashes in the room and makes Inka seem real. Even more scary than the storm, though, was seeing Antwan yesterday.

I still can't believe Antwan was *crying*! He didn't want me to see, but I did. He was hurt, too, like he'd been in a fight. And mad. He kicked one of Rock's barber chairs and yelled really loud. Rock was talking calm, telling Antwan to let it go. Made me think of that song from *Frozen*. Charlie would sing that song all the time!

I put my arm around Charlie, and even though it makes no sense for her to leave Mama's bed to get in mine, it feels good that she feels safe with me. I fall asleep thinking about Antwan and hoping he's okay.

On the bus, Sneaky's real quiet. He doesn't joke around like he normally would.

"Is Antwan good?" I finally ask.

"He got jumped; how you think he is?"

"Dang," I say. "Who did it?"

Sneaky shrugs. "He ain't really talkin' about it. Moms is super mad, though."

I don't say anything. I know Mama would be mad, too, if something happened to me or Charlie, especially a fight.

"I think he was with some of his friends," I say, remembering something Antwan said last night. "They took off when the fight started."

"How you know that?" Sneaky asks.

"He said it," I say. "I was at the barbershop when Rock went out there."

"He got some punk friends, then!" Sneaky says angrily. "If that was you gettin' jumped on, I wouldn't run."

"I wouldn't run, either," I tell Sneaky. He grins a little and we do the candy boy shake.

"So you stayin' after school today?" Sneaky asks. "They got JFL practice."

Junior Football League. It's all Sneaky's been talking about lately, even more than his shoes!

"Nah," I say. "I got some stuff to do." I don't tell him it's poem stuff with Angel.

"Bro, we're all supposed to play!" Sneaky says. "You, me, Mike O, and Jules."

Yeah, we all talked about it last year, when we were just fifth graders, but I figured Sneaky would be too busy with his business to play a sport.

"You can catch and you kinda quick, so you could probably be a receiver; Mike O, too," Sneaky says. "I'm QB all day!"

Sneaky keeps talking about the team and who all's gonna be on it. When we get to school and pile off the bus, he asks me again.

"So you tryin' out, right?"

"Yeah," I say. "I guess."

But that all changes when I check my email during advisory and see a message from Ms. Marlee. She says I've been assigned a mentee and I'll meet him next week.

September 18

What I know about my mentee:

1. His name is Kobe Love.
2. He's in third grade.
3. He likes video games and basketball.
4. He sometimes acts up in class.

What I *didn't* know about my mentee:

1. He's the same kid with braids from the library who wouldn't sit still during story time!

I recognize him right away when I walk into Ms. Marlee's room for our first Rockets Reach Back meeting. You gotta be kidding me!

"Please don't tell me *that's* my mentor," the kid says, slapping his hand to his head like he's super devastated. "Yo, Ms. Marlee, I don't even *need* a mentor!"

Tayshaun shakes his head, and Angel goes, "Oh snap!" They both look super glad this Kobe kid ain't their mentee.

"Kobe, Isaiah is your assigned mentor, just like we discussed. And I hope you haven't forgotten what we said about speaking respectfully."

Kobe sighs extra loud, then walks over and holds out his hand. I shake it without saying anything.

"Very nice to meet you, Isaiah. I look forward to being your mentee," he says. This dude sounds like he's reading a brochure! He turns to Ms. Marlee and asks, "Was that aight?"

"Much better," Ms. Marlee says. "Isaiah, we are *very* glad to have you here with us."

When Ms. Marlee tells us all to take a seat, I feel like walking right out the door. We're supposed to sit by our mentees, and Kobe's slouched in his chair like he doesn't want to be here. Tayshaun's mentee is a little older, and he just looks bored. Angel's mentee, Zani, scoots her chair super close to her, so close their arms are touching. She reminds me of Charlie.

"Today is all about getting to know each other," Ms. Marlee says. "Take a few minutes and tell each other two special things about yourselves."

Kobe's talking before Ms. Marlee even finishes her sentence.

"Video games," he says. "I can beat anybody in any game, any time. And I'm gonna be in the NBA, just like the other Kobe."

I snicker, and Kobe narrows his eyes.

"What? You got somethin' to say cuz I'm short?"

I mean, he *is* kinda short. Looks like the ball would bounce higher than him!

"Nope," I say with a shrug. "You can be short, as long as you're good."

"I'm good," Kobe says. "So whatchoo like to do?"

"I'm a writer," I say. "And I got my own business."

"The business part is cool." Kobe shrugs. "But writing? Nah."

"Writing takes skill," I say. Kobe makes a face like he doesn't believe me. That's aight. If he stays my mentee, he'll definitely find out.

Kobe complains about almost every activity Ms. Marlee has us do. Not gonna lie; I'm thinking maybe he shouldn't be a part of Rockets Reach Back. It should be for kids who *want* to be a part of it, like Angel's mentee. The two of them are actually smiling and laughing; Kobe looks like he just got teeth pulled. The only time he perks up is when we have to throw a ball around while we answer questions. Honestly, the best part of the whole meeting is the pizza we get to eat at the end, but Kobe even complains about that!

Maybe Sneaky was right; playing football would be way more fun than this.

September 19

"Long time, no see!" Mr. Shephard calls with a wave. Since school started, the library has been extra busy. Mr. Shephard is on the go, no time to stop and talk to me about this Kobe kid. So I just wave and head to the GD room, hoping he's free soon. I'm supposed to be at the barbershop, but Rock called and told me he had some things to do today. Everybody's busy, I guess.

Man, even the GD room is filled. Mostly kids on the computers, but there's a girl reading a book in *my* spot! I sit on an orange beanbag instead, but since I don't feel like writing anymore, I just read from one of Daddy's notebooks and let his words tell mine to come on out.

I turn to a page where Daddy wrote that words are like oxygen—you really live when you breathe them in. I think he was right.

I keep reading Daddy's words and wish he was here to talk to me about writing. I know he loved to write stories and I love poems, which are a little different, but I bet we could've done a lot of writing together. Why didn't I know all this sooner? It's like Daddy kept his writing a secret, but why? After I read for a while, I get an idea for a poem.

HIDING

Maybe Daddy was hiding
His words just like a treasure,
And maybe the more I read them,
I'll start to know him better.
My daddy was a hero,
with words as superpowers,
Cuz even though he's gone,
They're blooming just like flowers.

Once I finish writing, I go back to the children's section to find Mr. Shephard. He's still busy, but I decide I'll help him with the books he's shelving.

"So how's middle school treating you?" he asks me.

"Okay, I guess," I say. "It's different, though. And you know that little kid who comes here and gives you a hard time? The one with braids?"

Mr. Shephard thinks for a second, then cracks up. "You must be talking about Kobe. He's a good kid."

Good kid?

"Mr. S, are we talking about the same Kobe? The one who won't stop talking during story time and always complains about *everything*?"

"Yep, that's Kobe!" Mr. Shephard says with a chuckle. "And yes, past all of that, he's a good kid."

I tell Mr. S about the Rockets Reach Back thing and how Kobe acts like he doesn't even want to be in it.

"I think Ms. Marlee's forcing him to do it," I say. "She must have some good dirt on him."

"Sounds like the program is just what he needs," Mr. Shephard says. "And he's got the perfect mentor."

I shake my head. Usually Mr. S knows what he's talking about, but with this, I'm not so sure.

"I don't know about all that," I say. "He doesn't even like me."

"Oh, I guarantee he likes you," Mr. Shephard says, shelving the last few books. "Try this at your next meeting."

Mr. Shephard starts to tell me what I should do with Kobe, but then a few kids and their mom come up to ask him about some action series and he gets busy with them. I wait for as long as I can, but Mama comes to pick me up and I have to leave without Mr. S's advice.

September 21

"What are *you* doing here?"

The words fly out of my mouth before I can stop them because I'm shocked to see Antwan in the barbershop, cleaning Rock's clippers. That's *my* job!

"None of your business," Antwan says with a scowl. He puts the clippers down and calls to Rock.

"Yo, I'm done with these, can I go now?"

Rock closes the supply-closet door and tosses a rag to Antwan, and one to me, too.

"How you doin', li'l man?" he says. "Let's get those windows sparklin', aight, fellas? Got special guests coming in."

I catch the rag, still wondering what's going on and why Antwan's here. We spray the windows in silence, moving out of the way whenever more customers come in. Then I'm sweeping up the black clouds of hair, and Antwan's spraying clippers like crazy. I think winning the competition has made Rock the busiest barber in town!

One thing I notice about today is that Rock keeps calling Antwan over to watch what he's doing when he cuts hair.

"The comb is your friend, your navigation system," Rock tells Antwan while he gives this dude a taper. "And you wanna make sure you hold the clippers like this so you get the angle you want."

Antwan leans against an empty chair and crosses his arms, but I can tell he's paying attention.

When Mama comes to pick me up, Rock hands me a ten-dollar bill. I see him give Antwan one, too.

"Isaiah, your mom is gonna drop Antwan off at home. Already talked to her about it. Good work today, both of you. Antwan, I'll see you tomorrow after school, right?"

Antwan flips his hood over his head and nods. He walks out to Mama's car without even saying goodbye.

"Why's he even here?" I ask Rock.

"Community service," Rock says.

"He's in trouble?" I ask. I mean, I know Antwan's kinda bad, but I didn't know he got arrested or anything. Rock shakes his head, though.

"Nah, he's not in trouble," he says. "He's on his way *out* of trouble. Now don't keep your mama waiting."

On the ride home I think about how Rock wants to start his own barber school. I wonder if Antwan knows he's the first student.

September 25

Our second Rockets Reach Back meeting isn't much better than the first. Kobe still complains for basically the whole time. When Ms. Marlee says we're gonna read a book to each other and Kobe says her idea sucks, Ms. Marlee raises an eyebrow and says, "Do I need to call your grandmother, Kobe?"

Kobe thinks for a second before he mumbles, "No."

"Good," Ms. Marlee says. "I think one phone call today is enough, don't you?"

A few other mentees snicker. Kobe stares at his shoes and doesn't say anything else. I almost feel bad for him. *Almost.*

"So what kind of books do you like?" I ask when Ms. Marlee

tells us we can pick one from her book bin. Kobe shrugs. We watch Zani race over and grab a Sofia Martinez book, and Tayshaun's mentee, Marcus, gets *Diary of a Wimpy Kid*.

"You ready to pick one?" I ask again. Kobe shakes his head and crosses his arms.

"I ain't picking no stupid book," he says.

"Yeah, but we have to," I say. "And it sounds like you already got in trouble today, right?"

"So?" Kobe says. "My teacher is dumb."

"Why you think that?" I ask.

"Cuz."

Since Kobe's not moving toward the books, I go and grab one about a ninja.

"Here," I say.

"Boring!" Kobe says, rolling his eyes.

"It doesn't matter," I say. "We still gonna read it."

It's a rhyming book, which is cool. At first, Kobe's making comments under his breath and moving around, but he's quiet by the time I turn to the last page.

"That was pretty good, right?" I ask. Kobe yawns real loud and stands up.

"Ms. Marlee, are we done now? Can we go?"

"Remember, Kobe, we have an hour together," Ms. Marlee says. "Looks like you and Isaiah are ready to move on to the next activity."

"Nooo," groans Kobe. He does it under his breath, though, so Ms. Marlee doesn't hear. "The next activity should be going home!"

"Man, why you always do this?" I ask.

"Cuz I don't wanna be here," Kobe says with a shrug.

"Yeah. We all know!"

This kid is getting on my nerves and I'm nowhere near as calm as Mr. S. The whole thing feels like a waste of time.

I make sure to tell Ms. Marlee that as soon as the meeting is over and Kobe jets out the door.

"I know it's frustrating, Isaiah," Ms. Marlee says. "But just keep your eyes open. Try to find out more about Kobe's story. And remember—your mentee needs you. We matched you with Kobe for a specific reason."

"What's the reason?" I ask. To me, this ain't a match at all!

"Keep watching," Ms. Marlee says with a cryptic smile. "You'll see."

I try asking again, super nice, but Ms. Marlee doesn't tell me. I sigh and leave her classroom. It doesn't help that once I'm in the hallway, Angel goes on and on about her mentee.

"Zani is so sweet! Look what she made me!" Angel dangles a homemade string necklace with a heart on it. She must notice the look on my face, cuz she stops running her mouth to ask me, "What's wrong with you?"

"Really, Angel? You haven't seen my mentee?" I ask. I never

thought I'd say this, but I'd rather deal with *ten* Charlies than one Kobe.

"He's cute; what's the problem?"

"Cute? Nah, Angel. He's a terror! He don't even want to be there!"

"None of them really do, I guess," Angel says. "But we have to make them want to be."

"You can't make someone—" I start to disagree with Angel, but she cuts me off.

"Look at us, though! I mean, Ms. Marlee didn't make us be friends, did she?"

I don't say anything at first, probably because I hate when Angel's kinda right.

"You and him will be fine," Angel says. "Maybe if you act more like me, your mentee will like you."

"Ha ha ha, very funny," I say.

"I'm just playing; relax!" Angel laughs.

We have a few minutes before our rides get here so we put finishing touches on our birthday card for Angel's dad. The whole time, though, I'm thinking about flipping through Daddy's notebooks to see if he has any advice on how to handle a kid like Kobe.

"Yo, if that was me, I'd give that kid the deuces!" Sneaky says. Me and him are playing Madden, which he swears is the same as practicing football.

"All y'all do is talk all day?" Sneaky asks, throwing a long pass to his receiver.

"Yeah, and do these activities," I tell him. I tackle his guy just before he gets to the end zone. "But Ms. Marlee says we're gonna take some field trips and stuff."

"Bro, if you woulda joined the team, you'd be taking field trips all the time!" Sneaky says, shaking his head.

On the next play, Sneaky's quarterback runs it in for a touchdown, and he lifts his arms in the air.

"That's exactly what I'm gonna do tomorrow!" he tells me. "You comin' to my game, right?"

"Of course!" I say.

"Good," Sneaky says. "You can talk to Coach A or Coach Kwame. Maybe it's not too late to get on the team."

I knew Sneaky was gonna say something about playing football. He'll probably be upset that I'm not playing, but I gotta tell him.

"Nah, I'm good on football."

"Huh?" Sneaky turns to look at me, and that gives my guy a chance to run the ball back to the thirty-five-yard line.

"You really not gonna play?" Sneaky asks.

"I won't have time," I say. "Tuesdays and Thursdays, I'm at the shop, plus the mentor thing on Mondays. I barely have time for my business!"

Truth is, I'm not even supposed to be playing video games with Sneaky right now. Angel's making some kind of catalog of our cards, and I still have a Thanksgiving poem to write.

"Aight, bro, do you," Sneaky says with a shrug. "Guess you gonna be Ms. Marlee Junior, huh?"

"Yeah, right," I say. "I don't wanna do this whole mentor thing anyway!"

"Then why you doing it?" Sneaky asks. He makes his voice all sing-songy. "Cuz Angel said to?"

"Nah, bro!" I say quickly.

"Then why?"

It hits me that I really don't have an answer. Maybe I'm doing Rockets Reach Back cuz it seems like the right thing to do. Mama was all proud when I told her about it, and I know Daddy would be proud, too. In all the stories he wrote, Isaiah Dunn is a superhero who saves the day. The more I read, the more I feel like I gotta be a hero in real life. But to a kid like Kobe? I'm not sure that's possible.

"I'm just sayin', don't waste your time if you don't even wanna do it," Sneaky tells me. Him scoring another touchdown on me is like an exclamation point. He's right; there are plenty of other ways to be a hero.

September 30

I'm shocked to see Angel at Sneaky's first football game, but it turns out that Coach A is her *dad*! I guess it works out, though, cuz we can do business stuff while we watch Sneaky play. Well, while *I* watch Sneaky play. Angel's not into football.

"It's a good thing you're here, or I'd be stuck watching that," Angel says when we find seats on the bleachers. "My daddy played, my big brother plays, and football makes absolutely *no* sense. Run, knock somebody down, get back up, and do it again. It's like little kids!"

"Are you serious? Football's like poetry in motion!"

I heard Daddy say that once, while we were watching a game together. He said that when everybody on the field does what they're supposed to, it's just like how words come together in a poem.

"OMG, you sound real corny right now." Angel smirks and holds up her notebook. "Just make sure your poetry is on the page, aight?"

"It always is; it's always tight. I'm always Dunn, and always right!" I say, giving her a smirk of my own. "Poetry in motion!"

I crack up and watch the game while Angel shakes her head and gets back to writing my words with her gel pens. If they gave an award for best handwriting, Angel would win easily. And if they gave an award for best eleven-year-old quarterback, Sneaky just might get it. When he's video-game bragging, he says he got perfect vision of the field. Right now, it looks like he was telling the truth.

"Ugh, he always gotta do the most," Angel says after Sneaky completes a pass for a touchdown and does the candy boy shake.

"Stop hatin'," I say. "That was a perfect throw!"

"Great, now you can come up with a perfect poem," Angel says, pointing to my notebook. It's in my lap, but I haven't opened it yet. Since her dad really liked the card we made him, Angel's been hounding me to write more and more birthday poems.

"Just for you, Angel, I'm gonna write a football birthday poem," I say. "I hope you can draw something good to go with it."

"Boy, please!"

Angel gets out green, white, and brown colored pencils and starts practicing her footballs. I write the football birthday poem and one about turning real old, all by halftime. Angel's practice drawings are really good; all we gotta do is buy more of that card paper and transfer our ideas over. For now, though, Angel has other ideas.

"It's a lotta people out here," she says, looking around. "Quick! Go see if you can borrow Sneaky's helmet!"

"What?" I ask.

"Go borrow Sneaky's helmet while they do the halftime stuff," Angel says. "And start thinking up poems about winning or something."

Now I get what Angel's thinking. There's a whole bunch of YouTube videos of kids singing or playing the guitar at the mall or outside somewhere. People drop money in a hat for them, and then they get discovered. Well, me and Angel do the same thing, only with poems. We call it Poems on the Spot. I'll make up a poem, and Angel writes it really fast and super neat. At first I didn't think it would work, but a lot of times people give us money if the poem is good.

I hurry down the bleachers just as Sneaky's running to the sidelines for halftime, his helmet in one hand.

"Yo, Sneaky, you killin' it out there!" I say.

"I know, right! These guys are trash!"

"Sneaky, huddle up!" calls Angel's dad.

"See you after we finish stompin' them," Sneaky says, about to jog off.

"Hold up!" I say. "Can I borrow your helmet real quick? I'll bring it right back."

"What?" Sneaky looks at me like I asked for his passing arm.

"We need it just for a few minutes," I tell him. "I'll bring it to you before you start playing again."

"Who's we?" Sneaky asks, giving me a look and crossing his arms.

"I'll explain later; can I just borrow it?"

Sneaky hesitates. Angel's dad yells for him again. He hands me the helmet before running off.

"Hurry up, bro, and you betta bring it right back!"

Sneaky's helmet is hot and sweaty—gross!—and I bet Angel's gonna make the biggest stank face when she sees it. Oh well!

We set up near where people are selling food and snacks, and even though I always get nervous when we do this, I take a deep breath and make my voice nice and strong:

Never give up
When winning is close.
That's the time
You're needed the most.
Give it your best
But don't give it up.
If you keep trying,
You'll be strong enough.

I speak slowly so Angel has time to write it all down. Her pen flies across the fancy paper. A few people clap and toss change into the helmet. One lady calls out, "Perfect message for the Sharks! Maybe next time!" The Sharks are the team Sneaky's playing against, so she's clowning them. Angel jumps on it quick.

"Would you like a copy of the poem?" she asks the lady, holding up the final paper. Hopefully the lady has a kid on Sneaky's team and wants something to remember from the game.

The lady looks at the paper and laughs.

"My sister's son plays for the Sharks; I'ma give this to her!" She drops a few dollars into the helmet and goes on to get her snacks.

"Do another one," Angel says, eyeing a group of people in football jerseys. "Something about the Lions."

I think hard and put my words together quick. The group stops to listen, and more money clinks inside the helmet.

"Do one about popcorn!" someone calls out. I say a short poem, and Angel writes it and cuts it out using those squiggly scissors so it kinda looks like a piece of popcorn. I do one more poem before I realize the crowd is getting smaller. I hear a whistle and my heart stops.

"Yo, I gotta get this helmet to Sneaky!" I say. I dump the money into her bag, which maybe we shoulda used in the first place, and take off toward the field. When I get to Sneaky, he's sitting on the bench, a mad look on his face. I hold out the helmet and he snatches it.

"Coach made me sit cuz I didn't have my helmet," he says.

"My bad, Sneaky. Me and Angel were doing the business and it was real cool," I try to explain.

"The poem stuff?" Sneaky asks, wrinkling his nose. "I thought you were here to watch my game."

"I am!" I say.

"Whatever," Sneaky says. He jams his helmet on and turns away from me.

"What's wrong with you?" Angel asks when I get back to our seats in the bleachers.

"Nothing."

I watch Sneaky play for the rest of the half, which means Angel's trippin' cuz I'm not writing poems. It's starting to feel like no matter what I do, neither of my friends is happy.

October 2

I'm the first one to Ms. Marlee's room after school, and my stomach's karate-chopping like crazy! I feel bad that Ms. Marlee's smiling so big when I come in. She has no idea what I'm about to say next.

"Good to see you, Isaiah!" Ms. Marlee says. "Once everyone gets here, we'll break off into pairs. Kobe would probably enjoy going to the gym if you don't mind shooting hoops with him."

"Ummm, Ms. Marlee, I kinda got something to tell you," I say.

"What's up?"

"Ummm, I think I have to stop doing the Rockets Reach Back thing," I say. I tell her about my business and my barbershop job, and school and homework and my friends and stuff.

"That does sound busy, but I was counting on your commitment here," Ms. Marlee says. I swallow hard.

"I know. But . . ." I pause, cuz I don't know how to tell her the whole thing feels like a waste of time.

"Is it Kobe?" Ms. Marlee asks.

I let out my breath. How did she know? "Yeah, kinda," I say. "It's like he doesn't even want to be here. He complains all the time, no matter what activity you have us do. How am I supposed to help him not get in trouble? He doesn't even listen to me when we're here!"

Ms. Marlee smiles. "Kobe's tough, but he's an amazing kid."

"He's annoying! Like my little sister, Charlie. Maybe it would be cool if he was like Zani or Marcus."

"But he's not, and that makes him special," Ms. Marlee says. "I'd love it if you gave him another chance, but if you do decide to leave the program, I appreciate you letting me know now, so I can find Kobe a new mentor."

"Hold up! You're not gonna be my mentor anymore?"

Ms. Marlee and I whirl around and see Kobe standing in the doorway, his book bag hanging off his shoulder and a confused look on his face.

"Well, Kobe, Isaiah has a really busy schedule and so he might need to—" Ms. Marlee tries to explain, but Kobe cuts her off.

"Nah, I get it," Kobe says, nodding. "You don't wanna be my mentor. It's cool."

"No, it's not that," I say. Kobe gives me a look like he knows it *is* that.

71

"Ms. Marlee, can I go home now?" he asks.

"Kobe, you're still here for an hour," Ms. Marlee says. "And I think you'll get to show off your basketball skills today."

Kobe's not excited like I thought he would be. He walks over to a chair, drops his bag on the floor, and sits down. I sit beside him, and there's an awkward silence for a while until Zani, Marcus, and the other mentees come in. Tayshaun, Angel, and the other mentors are right behind them. I think Angel's still kinda mad from Saturday cuz she doesn't say hi like she normally does. Tayshaun's the only one who even speaks to me!

"So who's your favorite player?" I ask Kobe, trying to sound upbeat when I don't feel it at all.

"Myself," Kobe says, not even looking at me. *Dang.*

The meeting drags on forever. Kobe's not his usual annoying self, and even when we shoot free throws after, it's like he's not really into it.

When Mama picks me up, she immediately asks me what's wrong.

"Nothing," I say.

"Nothing?" Mama gives me a look. "Now I know what nothing is, and that ain't it."

"I'm just tired," I say. Just like that, a big yawn comes out. They say yawns are contagious, and that must be true, cuz Mama's yawning next.

"You and me both!" she says. "I told Miz Rita I would pick up pizza for dinner."

"You okay, Mama?" I ask. Mama hardly ever orders pizza; she always gets the frozen ones from the store.

"I'm like you, baby," she says. "Busy and tired! But don't worry, I'm gonna keep pushing and be just like my superhero son!"

Mama grins at me and I try to grin back. But I definitely don't feel like a superhero.

I feel like I'm letting everyone down.

October 3

BAM!!

"You wrong and you know it!"

Angel slams her lunch tray on the table so hard, both me and Sneaky jump. This is becoming one of her bad habits!

"Dang, why you always doing that?" Sneaky says, glaring at her.

"Whatchoo mean?" I ask, keeping my eyes glued to the French fries on my plate.

"You *know* what I mean," Angel says. When I look up at her, her hands are on her hips and her eyes are narrowed to tiny slits. "You really quit Rockets Reach Back?"

"Man, chill with all that," Sneaky says before I can answer. "He didn't want to do it, so he's not!"

Angel ignores Sneaky and keeps mean-mugging me.

"So you just gonna leave Kobe hangin'?" she asks.

"He don't even wanna be there," I say. "You must not see how he be giving me a hard time!"

I know what I'm saying is true, but that karate-chopping feeling is happening in my stomach. I really didn't think I was leaving him hanging . . . but he did look pretty sad yesterday.

"You don't get it," Angel says, shaking her head. "It's not supposed to be about us; it's about our mentees!"

Sneaky cracks up laughing, even spits out some of his milk!

"Who are you—Ms. Marlee?" He makes his voice sound like Angel's: "It's about our mentees!"

"Wow." Angel shakes her head, grabs her tray, and walks away.

"Bye!" Sneaky yells after her. Suddenly, I don't even want my fries anymore.

After school, instead of going to the barbershop, I walk to Fuller Field with Sneaky for his football practice. It turns into a setup, cuz Sneaky starts telling Coach A, Angel's dad, that I wanna be on the team!

"Okay, Word Man, let's see what else those hands can do," Coach A says, and before I can tell him the truth—that I don't want to play football—he has me running up and down the field a million times while he throws hard, spiral passes that I'm sup-posed to catch! I drop a bunch of them, and by the time the rest of the team gets here, my lungs are exploding and my legs feel like cooked spaghetti noodles.

"Yo, Isaiah, you joining the team?" asks Mike O. "'Bout time!"

I'm too busy catching my breath to answer him.

Coach A tosses me a water bottle (I catch it) and tells me to take a break on the bench so I can watch what an actual practice looks like. I watch for a while, then end up playing catch with one of Angel's little brothers. Angel doesn't talk about her family too much, but I know she's got two sisters and three brothers, who are all obsessed with football, like her dad. The one I'm playing catch with is only, like, five or six, but he's already really good. And unlike Kobe, he doesn't run his mouth all the time. The way he runs and squints and throws is just like a mini Coach A. I guess me and this kid got a lot in common; we both wanna be like our dads.

When practice is done, Sneaky races over, super excited.

"Yo, I think he likes you! If you were trash, he'd tell you to leave the field," Sneaky says. "We're gonna smash everybody if we play together! And we can do the candy boy shake after every touchdown! Did he say you can still join?"

"Uhhh," I say. My brain freezes because even though playing football with Sneaky would be pretty cool, I know it's not what I really want to do right now.

Sneaky stares at me for a second, then sighs.

"I get it. You not gonna play, are you?" he says.

"Maybe next year, Sneaky," I tell him.

"I knew it!" Sneaky says. "Bet you rather be doing all that poem stuff, huh?"

"Yeah, I would," I say. "I love words the way you love football."

"It's cool, I guess," Sneaky says. "I'm just sayin', our touchdown dance would've been *epic*!"

"It's already epic," I say. "All we gotta do is keep adding to it."

Sneaky nods, and I can tell he's coming up with something.

"Yo, let's try this," he says.

Sneaky fakes a throw, I fake a catch, and then we launch the *real* candy boy shake.

"Aight, so you wanna know what I do after football practice?" Sneaky asks.

"What?" I say, thinking he's gonna say something about going to the store to buy candy.

"I run all the way home," he says instead.

"Sneaky, you serious?" I ask. I don't think my legs can take any more running.

"Yeah, I'm serious! On your mark . . ."

"Hold on, bro, I'm tired!"

"Get set!"

"Sneaky, hold up!"

"GO!!!"

October 4

SWACK!

"So first you quit Rockets Reach Back, and then you go to a *football* practice?"

Me and Angel have art together, and today she slams her notebook on our table at the beginning of class. It's just as loud as when she drops her lunch tray on the table.

"Angel, chill," I groan. "It's not a big deal."

"Yeah, okay," Angel says, plopping down in the chair beside me. I'm starting to think it was a bad idea to pick seats next to each other. Angel's quiet for a second, but not for long.

"My dad says you really outta shape," Angel tells me. "He's super hard on his players, so are you sure you wanna do football?"

"Why you hatin', Angel? I can try football if I want to."

"Quiet down, Angel and Isaiah," says Mrs. Scott, our art teacher. "You'll need to hear the directions for today's project."

Me and Angel sigh at the same time, and I know we're thinking the same thing. That's basically all we heard last year in fifth grade with Mrs. Fisher: *"Quiet down, Angel and Isaiah!"* We get along much better now, but it's not always easy.

We're doing real sand art today, and Mrs. Scott has us pick either warm or cool colors to work with. Angel grabs the warm colors, and I go with cool. She picks the tall, curvy container, and I choose the short, round one. I'm thinking about how different me and her are—maybe *too* different. But then Mrs. Scott gives us free time once we're finished, and me and Angel both reach for our notebooks. It reminds me that we also got some things in common.

"Yours looks like a waterfall," Angel says.

"Yours looks like burning hot lava," I tell her.

"Bet you gonna write a poem about it, huh?"

"Maybe."

"Party invitations."

"Huh?"

Angel taps her notebook with her pink pen.

"That's what we should get into next," she says. "My auntie is planning my little cousin's birthday, and she was showing my mom all these party invitation ideas. Just think about how many birthday parties people have every week! We could sell invitations!"

"You sound like Sneaky," I say, shaking my head. She makes a face, but it's the truth. He's the only other person who talks and thinks business all the time like that. At least, he *used* to. It's much more football talk now.

"You just had to kill the vibe, huh?" Angel says. "Look, just think about it, okay? Invitations would be good for business."

The bell rings, and Angel's gone before I can say that the whole greeting card idea was cool at first, but now the business is too . . . business-y. All the poems I've written lately have been for cards, not for fun. When I read Daddy's notebook, my words start flowing and I can write whatever I want. With the cards, I'm stuck writing what *Angel* wants. Maybe things will change once we start selling a bunch of cards. For now, I guess I gotta come up with some party invitation poems.

October 6

Miz Rita cooks fried chicken and mashed potatoes for dinner, which me and Charlie are super happy about. Mama's been buying pizza every night cuz it's quick and easy. To be honest, I don't wanna see another slice for at least a few months! It's almost as bad as the beans and rice we were eating for days when we lived in the Smoky Inn.

"Miz Rita, this is the best food ever!" Charlie says with her mouth full of mashed potatoes. "Magnificent!"

There she goes with her big words. She'll hear them on TV or something, and then she's saying them all day and night. And I hate when she goes on and on about what Miz Rita does! I'm always hoping it don't make Mama feel bad. This time, it seems like Mama's okay.

"Yes, we really appreciate the change from pizza," Mama tells Miz Rita.

"Anytime, Lisa," Miz Rita says. "I told you that I can just cook like I always do. Don't feel like you gotta make meals on top of everything else you doing."

"You doing so much already," Mama says, shaking her head. "The least I can do is cook for my babies. I'll get us out your hair real soon."

Miz Rita sighs, but doesn't say anything else about it.

"How was your day, Miss Charlie?" she asks.

"Magnificent!" Charlie says. "My friend Aria had a birthday, and she gave me two cupcakes! And we had music today, and I'm the best singer in the whole class!"

I snort when Charlie says that. If she's the best singer, the class must be horrific! I've heard her sing, and it ain't pretty! I groan when Charlie launches into this song she's been learning. Of course, Mama and Miz Rita clap and whistle like she's Beyoncé. Why do grown-ups do that?

"And what about you, Isaiah? How's middle school treating you?" Miz Rita asks.

"It's fine," I say.

"Give her a little more than that, 'Saiah," Mama says.

I think about Kobe and Rockets Reach Back for a quick second, but I can't tell them that I quit. Or about how Kobe's face looked at the end of the meeting.

"My classes are normal," I say. "The teachers give too much homework."

"Nothing wrong with homework!" Miz Rita says. "Keeps your mind busy with the right things!"

Adults always say stuff like that, like all kids need is a boatload of homework to make them behave. I'd rather have my mind busy with writing poems than with geography or multiplying fractions.

After dinner, Miz Rita reads to Charlie while me and Mama do homework at the kitchen table. I read to Mama about the Mayan civilization, and she reads me a page from her huge textbook about how businesses can have an identity . . . or something like that.

"You probably think this is boring, huh?" Mama chuckles.

"Yeah, maybe a little," I say. "But it also makes me think about my business."

"Oh yeah?" Mama asks.

"Yeah, like, what do you do if the identity of your business changes and you don't really want it to?"

"Okay, 'Saiah, I know I saw you nodding off, but I guess you were paying attention!" Mama says. "I think if your business is changing and you don't want it to, you have to look at things from the inside out. What is the heart and purpose of your business, and does that match with what you're doing now?"

I tell Mama about the greeting cards and party invitations and how our poetry business isn't really exciting anymore. She listens and nods and says "hmmm" a lot.

"I think you have to decide what *you* want to do with your poems, Isaiah," Mama tells me. "And once you do, you have to share that with Angel."

"That might be tough," I say.

"It might be," Mama agrees. "But you're built for tough. We both are."

Mama's definitely tough. I know she's working hard on more than just school and her job. She doesn't talk much about how she used to drink, but I know she's fighting to stay away from that. On her dresser, she keeps an old birthday card from Daddy that says, "To the Strongest Woman I Know." I think Mama uses his words as inspiration just like I do. I think it would be cool if my poems could do the same thing Daddy's words do—help people. Like, maybe one day some kid will find my notebooks. That would be amazing.

Mama yawns and highlights her last section. I fill in the last blank on my worksheet. We did good work tonight. I think Daddy would be proud.

October 10

I'm still getting used to Antwan being at the barbershop every time I come in. Unlike me, he's here every day after school. Also unlike me, he does more than just sweeping up and cleaning things. Today, when things slow down a little, Rock actually lets Antwan cut his hair! It's not like Rock has a lot of hair, but still!

"Remember, that comb is like your GPS," Rock tells Antwan. He's holding a mirror, watching as Antwan moves the clippers across his close-to-bald head.

"Comb? There's nothing to comb, man!" Antwan says with a laugh.

"Always somethin' to comb," Rock replies, ignoring Antwan's joke. "You just get used to holding that in your hand."

Antwan keeps cutting, and Rock says stuff like "Good," and "Yup, just like that." I can tell that Antwan's really concentrating and doesn't want to mess up. I wouldn't want to, either!

"Aight, check that out," Antwan says when he's finished. He's got this grin on his face like he did something amazing, when all he really did was take off the little bit of hair Rock had left.

"Yeah, that's a decent job," Rock says, nodding as he checks out all his angles.

I get the broom and pretend like I'm sweeping, even though there's not much on the floor. Antwan cracks up.

"Oh, you got jokes, too, Isaiah?" Rock shakes his head. "Watch; your next haircut gonna be just like mine!"

The three of us are still laughing and joking when the barbershop door opens and two guys Antwan's age come inside. They nod w'sup to Rock but don't speak to him.

"Yo, Ant, you ready to roll?" one of them asks.

Antwan glances at Rock, then over at the guys. He opens his mouth, but it's Rock who speaks up.

"Y'all here for cuts?" Rock asks.

"Nah," says the other guy. "Just here to get Ant."

"Antwan's still working," Rock says. He folds his arms across his chest. "So it's either an edge-up or an exit, gentlemen."

The boys look at Rock, then Antwan, then at each other.

"Catch you later," the first one says. They look over their shoulders as they leave, like Antwan's gonna suddenly follow them. Antwan sucks his teeth once they're gone.

"Yo, you ain't have to do that," he says. "Those are my boys!"

"I know," says Rock, tossing a can of clipper spray to Antwan. "The same friends who bounced while you were getting beat up, remember?"

"It wasn't like that," Antwan mumbles. Rock doesn't say anything. He doesn't have to.

When Antwan goes to the bathroom, I ask Rock if he's trying to turn Antwan into a barber.

"I can't turn nobody into nothing," Rock says. "He got the skills, for sure. But all I can do is show him one path he could take. He gotta do the walking himself."

"Maybe he's, like, your first student," I say. "For your school."

"Maybe," Rock says. "And a good teacher never gives up on his student, right?"

Rock winks and hands me the dustpan. It feels super heavy when I grab it, and deep down, I'm thinking about Kobe and how maybe I shouldn't have given up on him.

October 15

"Charlie, you gotta keep your eyes open when the ball comes, okay?"

Charlie nods, but she still squeals and squeezes her eyes shut when I toss her the football.

We're playing catch outside the apartment while Mama writes a paper inside. Mama's always writing something these days, and even though it's different from me and Daddy's writing, it's still words. We're a family of words, I guess, and Charlie's up next. Hopefully she'll be better with writing than she is with catching a football!

"How 'bout you just throw to me," I say, after Charlie lets the ball hit her on the shoulder two times in a row. I walk over to show Charlie how to hold the football to throw a nice pass. She's concentrating real hard, and I have to swat her hand to keep her from sucking on her fingers.

"You gonna get the ball all slimy," I say. "That's disgusting!"

"Sorry," Charlie says. She grips the football like I said and tosses me a wobbly pass.

"It's heavy, 'Saiah!" she says, throwing the next pass with both hands.

When her next throw lands a few feet in front of me and bounces further away, Charlie hangs her head.

"I'm not good at anything, 'Saiah," she says, all sad.

"What? That ain't true, Charlie," I say. I run to pick up the ball, and Charlie's still staring at the ground when I get over to her.

"We can play something else if you want," I say. "Wanna go to the playground?"

"No, cuz I'll probably be bad over there, too!" Charlie says. "Brianna from my class said I'm stupid."

"Charlie, you know that isn't true, so you don't even have to get all upset," I say.

"But she always says stuff like that," Charlie tells me. "Whenever I read at story time she says mean things to me or throws her books on the floor. Mrs. Woods has to call her mom a lot."

"Sheesh, sounds like Kobe," I say under my breath.

"Who?" asks Charlie.

"Nobody," I say. I don't know why that kid keeps popping into my mind! Also, I keep thinking about some of the stuff Ms. Marlee told us in our meetings, like that there could be something else going on with someone if they're being mean. Charlie actually listens when I tell her that, and if Sneaky could see me now, he'd definitely call me Ms. Marlee Junior.

"She always gets mad when it's time to read our books," Charlie continues. "Maybe she doesn't like to read."

"Maybe she can't read that good, and she's mad that you can," I say.

"Ohhh, then she should just practice!" Charlie says. She swipes the football from me and grins. "Can we go to the playground now?"

"Yeah," I say, glad she's happy again.

I chase her to the playground and tackle her, but not too hard. She does the swings and slide while I write a quick poem about bullies. Then Charlie wants to try catch again. She does a lot better.

When I'm lying in bed that night, listening to Mama read Charlie a bedtime story, I start thinking about the mean girl in her class. I wonder what Daddy would do about a bully. He'd probably do the same thing Ms. Marlee said—try to figure out how to help the bully *and* the person who's being bullied.

Then it hits me! Kobe acts just like Charlie's bully, so maybe he has the same thing going on! He doesn't like school, so maybe that's why he always gets in trouble and why he doesn't like Rockets Reach Back. And maybe I can still help, superhero style! I tell Inka my ideas and read Daddy's notebook until I fall asleep.

October 16

"Well, look who it is! Nice to see you, Isaiah," Ms. Marlee says when I burst into her classroom on Monday after school. I'm the first one here, just like last time.

"He can't read!" I exclaim. "That's it, isn't it, Ms. Marlee?"

Ms. Marlee stops straightening the chairs in her room and studies me. A small smile crosses her face, but a frown follows it.

"I'm going to assume you mean Kobe," she says. "Your former mentee."

Ouch. Hearing her say *former* kinda hurts. I swallow and ignore the karate-chopping in my stomach.

"Yeah, I was thinking about what you said and that maybe he can't read that good," I say. "Maybe that's why he gets in trouble."

"Isaiah, remember how I told you I paired you with Kobe for a reason?" Ms. Marlee asks. I nod. Ms. Marlee takes her hands and holds them apart. Then she slowly brings them together.

"I take a student who carries a notebook with him wherever he goes and pair him with a student who thinks reading should be outlawed. Does that seem unbelievable?"

At first I wanna say yeah, that it's the worst pairing ever, even worse than when me and Angel had to work on a poetry project together last year. But then I understand exactly what Ms. Marlee was trying to do. And I feel bad for messing it up.

"I guess it makes sense," I say. "Is it too late to help Kobe with his reading?"

"You can stick around to see if he shows up today, but he missed last week's meeting," Ms. Marlee tells me. "And he's still having classroom issues as well."

Ms. Marlee tells me that she has a student who can be Kobe's new mentor, but that Kobe hasn't shown up to meet him.

"He'd probably never say this, but deep down inside, Kobe was disappointed when you didn't stay."

Ouch again. I think about how Kobe looked when he found out I was quitting the program. Maybe he really did need me as his mentor. And maybe it's not too late.

"I can still help, Ms. Marlee," I say. "Can I be his mentor again?"

Some of the other kids start coming in, and there's more of them than before. I guess Rockets Reach Back is getting popular. Ms. Marlee watches them just like I do. No Kobe.

"I think it would be good for both of you," Ms. Marlee says. "I'll speak with Kobe's grandmother and mom and see if he'll come back."

"Okay," I tell her. I'm feeling kind of down because they might say no. Maybe if I could talk to him, tell him I'm sorry, he would wanna come back to the program.

Ms. Marlee says I can stay for the meeting, but I say no thanks. There's one place Kobe might be, and it won't hurt to check.

I walk as fast as I can to the library and ask Mr. Shephard if he's seen Kobe.

"He was here a little while ago," Mr. Shephard tells me. "He was waiting for his grandma to pick out her audiobooks."

"Thanks!" I say. I race around the children's section, check out the GD room, and even go upstairs. No Kobe. *Dang!* I must've missed him. I trudge back to the GD room and head to my spot by the window.

And that's when I see him.

There's a playground near the library, and I see a short kid with braids shooting hoops. I dash outside and over to the court.

"Yo, Kobe!" I call as I get closer. He stops shooting and stares at me.

"Hey," I say. Kobe just shakes his head and puts up another shot. Yikes! This is gonna be harder than I thought!

"I talked to Ms. Marlee today," I tell him.

"Good for you, Ghost Man!" Kobe says.

"Look, I'm sorry 'bout all that," I tell him. "I'm back in the program now."

"So?"

"So you should be, too," I say. "I want to be your mentor again."

"Man, that program sucks!" Kobe says. "Nobody wants to sit around and talk all day. I gotta work on my game!"

Kobe launches a shot that hits nothin' but net. I grab the ball.

"Stop playin'!" Kobe says, holding his hands out for the ball.

"How 'bout this," I say, taking some steps away from the basket. "If I hit a shot from back here, you come to Rockets Reach Back next week."

Kobe laughs. "And when you miss, you give me my ball and leave me alone!"

"Bet!"

Kobe snickers when I dribble the ball a few times. I'm not a basketball star or anything, but I hit plenty of shots when I play against Sneaky. I usually beat him, too. I'm just hoping this one goes in! Daddy named me after Isiah Thomas, the Pistons star from back in the day. And since I'm standing here with a Kobe, it's almost like the ball *has* to go in! I take a deep breath and shoot . . .

SWISH!

It feels real good to see that Kobe's grin is as big as mine.

October 18

SMACK!

Angel's pink notebook hits the floor by my feet, and since I'm so used to it now, I don't even flinch.

"Hey," I say.

"'Bout time you came to your senses," Angel says before shaking her head and sitting next to me.

We have a mentors-only meeting today, and I'm actually

excited about it. This will also give me a chance to talk to Angel about our business.

"What's all that?" Angel asks, nodding at my stuffed backpack.

"Books," I say. "For Kobe."

I went to the library yesterday, and Mr. Shephard gave me a bunch of recommendations for Kobe. He said a lot of kids don't like reading because they haven't found a book that they connect to. I guess he's kinda right. I was only reading Daddy's notebooks before Mr. S showed me some other books that were kinda cool. There's gotta be *something* in this stack that Kobe will like.

"Ummm, okay," she says. "You think he gonna like that?"

"I don't know. I hope so," I tell her.

"If he's anything like my little brothers, he won't."

"Dang, why you so negative?" I ask.

"I'm not negative, just statin' facts," Angel says with a shrug. "If he ain't into reading, he ain't gonna read those."

Some of the excitement I felt slips away, and I wonder if Angel's right. Well, even if she is, I'm still gonna try!

"It's a bunch of books that a *librarian* gave me, so I think he'll like at least one of them."

"Yeah, maybe," Angel says. She doesn't sound too convinced.

"How old is your brother?" I ask. "The one who plays football."

"Which one? They all do," Angel says.

"The little one?"

"My little brothers are six and eight," Angel says. "You were playing catch with C.J. He's six, always tagging along with my dad to practices."

Ms. Marlee picks that second to clap her hands to get our attention and lead us on our normal chant, where she says, "Rockets Fly High!" and we yell, "Rockets Reach Back!"

"Rockets Fly High!"

"Rockets Reach Back!"

"Rockets Reach Where?"

"ROCKETS REACH BACK!"

It's kinda corny, but we always get hyped and clap and cheer after the chant. It's even louder today, with twelve mentors instead of seven.

"Let's start with our breathing and stretches," Ms. Marlee says. We all know what she's gonna say next, so we say it with her:

"Cuz you don't live if you don't breathe, and you don't grow if you don't stretch!"

After we do some deep breathing and stretch our arms as high up as we can, Ms. Marlee has us put our chairs in a circle and asks for a volunteer to stand in the middle.

"Isaiah wants to!" Angel says loudly. I give her a look and elbow her, but Ms. Marlee is already waving me up to the middle.

"C'mon, Isaiah; consider this your welcome-back activity," she says with a smile.

I stand up in the middle of everybody and glare at Angel.

"Alright, Isaiah, I want you to slowly spin around so you can see everyone," Ms. Marlee says. I stay in the middle but do a 360 like I'm in Rock's barber chair. I know everybody's name except a few of the new people.

"Nice spinning; keep going!" Ms. Marlee says, and a few kids chuckle.

Maaannn, Ms. Marlee has me up here looking dumb!

"Now, everyone else, give him some information. Say your favorite color, show him your favorite number, tell him your middle name, make a silly face. Keep the information coming, and, Isaiah, pick a spot and stand still."

This time, I'm only facing four people, so I see Angel holding up one finger and Harmoni making her face look like a fish. I hear other stuff from everyone else, too.

"Twenty-four!"

"Yellow!"

"Jade!"

"Pizza and fries!"

"Spencer!"

Finally, Ms. Marlee tells us to stop.

"Alright, Isaiah, you can sit down. Did you get everything?"

"Huh?"

"Did you get all the information your team gave you? Tayshaun's middle name, Nisha's favorite food, Jalen's favorite number?"

"I mean, I got some of it, but not all."

"And why do you think that was?" Ms. Marlee asks everyone.

"Cuz he stopped spinning," Angel answers.

"I couldn't see everyone from the middle of the circle," I add. Ms. Marlee nods and smiles.

"You guys are probably figuring this out already, but it will be the same thing with your mentees. You won't always be able to catch everything, especially when you're in the middle of everything. Don't beat yourself up if you don't have all the answers or if things don't go exactly how you plan. Take in as much as you can."

It feels like Ms. Marlee is talking right to me, and my face gets hot. I look down at my bag of books and think about what Angel said. I have an amazing, superhero plan, but . . . what if Kobe doesn't like any of the books?

October 19

"I wanna go, too!"

Charlie's pouting, watching Mama read over the permission slip Ms. Marlee gave us yesterday. We're taking our first Rockets Reach Back field trip next week, and I wanna make sure my paper is turned in ASAP. There was this time last year when Mama kept forgetting to sign my permission slip for Laser Zone, this amusement center I really wanted to go to. I ended up stuck in Mr. Larry's class with all the other fifth graders who stayed at school.

"It's not fair! I wanna go!" Charlie whines.

"Chill, Charlie," I say. "This is only for kids in the program."

"But I wanna go to the children's museum!"

Charlie sticks two fingers in her mouth, which she knows I hate. I ignore her, which I know *she* hates.

"Well, it does look like they need a few parent chaperones," Mama says. "Maybe I could volunteer. They probably wouldn't mind if I brought your sister."

Charlie goes, "Yay!" at the exact same time that I go, "Nooo!"

"Mama, you don't have to volunteer," I say. But she's already grabbing her planner. She flips a few pages, then sighs.

"I have a group meeting that afternoon," Mama says. "Sorry, Charlie. We'll all go to the museum another time, okay?"

"But I wanna go with Isaiah!" Charlie says.

"You will!" I tell her. "Just not this time."

Man, I thought when Charlie started school she'd stop being so whiny. Guess not. Mama says it's normal for her to wanna do everything I do, but sometimes it can get annoying.

Mama signs the paper, and I go in my room to put it in my backpack. Charlie follows me, still sucking on those fingers.

"Yo, Charlie, you can't be in here with your fingers in your mouth," I tell her. She pulls them out and wipes them on her pants. Yuck!

"Why you do that, anyway?" I ask.

"Cuz I like to," Charlie says. She hops up on my bed. "I drew a picture of Inka."

"Cool."

"I'm a real good drawer, 'Saiah. The art lady, Ms. Lee, said so."

"Artist, Charlie. Not draw-er," I say. I take out my notebook to do some writing.

"Can I draw something in there?" Charlie asks. "It'll be real good!"

"Charlie, you have your own notebooks," I say. She's always drawing in mine, sometimes even drawing over my words!

"But I promise it'll look nice," she says. "Please?"

"Okay, you can draw a picture in my notebook, but if it's bad, I get to write in your princess notebook. A poem about you sucking your nasty fingers. Deal?"

"Okay!" Charlie squeals and runs to get her colored pencils. When she comes back she grabs my notebook and turns to an empty page.

"Charlie has some nasty fingers, always in her mouth. She puts them in when she can't win and things are going south!" I tease. I'm ready to roast her in this poem!

"Stop it, 'Saiah, that's mean!" she says, not taking her eyes off the page.

"It's true, though!" I say.

While I wait for Charlie to finish, I read from Daddy's notebook. In this story, superhero Isaiah Dunn has to find a Seeing Eye dog that's been stolen from an undercover agent. Isaiah eats a huge bowl of his mama's beans and rice in order to see through buildings. His super vision helps him find out where the thieves have hidden the dog. I'm almost at the end of the story when Charlie puts her drawing right in my face.

"Look, 'Saiah!" she says. "It's breathtaking!"

Charlie's real close to my face, so I almost say something about *her* breath, but I decide to be nice and just look at the picture.

"Whoa," I say. "Not bad."

Charlie drew a picture of a puppy with a cape around its neck. The puppy's brown, but his cape is, like, seven different colors. Charlie drew flowers, but they're in the sky, not on the ground. The sun she drew has a smiley face inside it, with pink sunbeams shooting out. Not gonna lie; dogs are hard to draw and I'm surprised Charlie's doesn't look hideous.

"I told you!" Charlie says. "That's Superdog, and he's gonna be my dog. I draw a picture of him every day!"

"Superdog?" I say, laughing. Li'l kids can be so corny!

"Does that mean you're not gonna write a poem about me?" Charlie asks.

"Yeah, yeah," I say. "I'll write one about Superdog instead."

"It betta be good, or he'll bite you!" Charlie says.

I chase Charlie out of my room, but I do start thinking about something. If Charlie had a dog, maybe she wouldn't bother me so much! I bet Mama would like a dog, too, especially if I tell her I have enough money to pay for it. Before I know it, I'm imagining what kind of dog it will be and what we'll name it. I open my notebook to write down name ideas and the first thing I see are my notes for working with Kobe at our next meeting:

1. Make him excited about the books
2. Let him pick
3. Play basketball after we read

It's a good plan, but since Rock always says you need a Plan C, D, and sometimes Z, I add a few more things, just in case.

October 23

"You reading *baby* books?"

Kobe makes a face as I pull a book from my backpack.

"Nah, it's just a book with pictures," I say. Mr. Shephard called them picture books, which makes sense, and he gave me a few of them along with the longer books for Kobe to read.

"You heard about this one?" I ask, holding up a book that has snowmen on the front.

"Nah," Kobe says.

"What about this one?" I ask, holding up a book called *Blackout*. "It's about a city that loses power at night."

"Nope!" Kobe turns and stares out the window. We're on the bus to the children's museum, and I thought it would be the perfect time to read. Guess not.

"My dad played for that school," Kobe says, pointing as we pass one of the schools downtown.

"For real? My mom goes there," I say.

"She play ball?" Kobe asks.

"No, she just goes to school."

"Oh."

Kobe's quiet for a minute, but then he starts right up again.

"I bet I'm better than everybody at your school," he says.

"Maybe," I say.

"Maybe? That's facts!" Kobe says. "I play every single day. My dad says you gotta do that to be good."

Kobe tells me his dad is playing basketball overseas.

"He's retiring soon, and when he gets home, he's gonna coach me. You lucky you know me now, cuz in a few years I'ma be famous!"

"Okay, Mr. Famous, which book you wanna read?" I ask, holding up both picture books.

"Neither," Kobe says. "Both boring."

"Aight," I say with a shrug. I open *Blackout* and start reading to myself. Mr. Shephard said that since Kobe looks up to me, it'll be good for him to see me reading and that it might make him want to read, too. I flip through the pages until we get to the museum, and Kobe doesn't look over at all.

"This place looks wack," Kobe groans.

"Trust me, it's not," I tell him. He doesn't look convinced.

All the other mentees are excited when we climb off the bus. The last time I came to the children's museum was with Mama and Charlie, and it was a really good day. Hopefully today will be, too.

Ms. Marlee reminds us to stay with our mentees and that we'll move from floor to floor all together. When we get inside, Kobe heads right to the Superhero exhibit. We take a test to see which Superhero we're most like, and I get Superman. Kobe gets Batman.

"That's what you should call me from now on," Kobe says.

"Okay, Batman, where we going next?"

Kobe wants to stay in the Hall of Justice, so we really don't see anything else on the first floor. It's cool, though, cuz we get to design our own superheroes and print a picture of them. I make an Isaiah Dunn who's holding a bowl of beans and rice. Kobe thinks it's corny, but I'm gonna glue the picture in Daddy's notebook. I have time to make a Superdog picture for Charlie, too. Kobe clowns it, but whatever.

We move upstairs and see a dinosaur exhibit, something

about butterflies, and the giant bubble exhibit that Charlie likes. Everything's going good until we get to the third floor.

Tony's one of the new mentees, and he's paired with Matthew, who's in seventh grade. When we get to a basketball exhibit, Kobe and Tony go head-to-head shooting baskets, and Kobe basically destroys Tony three times in a row! Tony doesn't like losing, so he wants rematch after rematch. I wander over to some other exhibits, but not for long. I hear some loud yelling and turn around just in time to see Kobe throwing the basketball at Tony and then knocking something over at another station.

I'm quick, but Ms. Marlee's quicker. She gets to Kobe first, and she takes him away to calm down. Mr. Pollard, who works at the elementary school, talks to Tony.

"What happened?" I ask Angel.

"I really don't know," Angel says, pointing to another arcade game. "Me and Zani were over there."

"Tony said something to Kobe, and then Kobe snapped!" Zani butts in.

"What he say?"

"He said 'at least I can read the word *basketball*,'" says Marcus. "And then Kobe got mad and hit him."

"He also called him HB," adds Nevaeh.

"HB?"

"Held back, cuz he doing the third grade over," explains Zani.

"Held back and still shorter than everyone else!" Nevaeh says with a laugh.

Zani starts to laugh, too, but Angel checks her real quick.

"Hey, cut that out. That ain't funny!" she says. "'Saiah, you better make sure he's okay."

Dang! I didn't know Kobe was held back. No wonder he got mad about what Tony said. I try to talk to him, but he stays with Ms. Marlee for the rest of our time at the museum. I don't even get to tell him that I know how he feels. When Angel used to tease me about smelling like smoke, I would get really mad, too. Maybe it would help Kobe if he knew all that.

But on the ride back, Kobe keeps his hood on and his fists balled up. He doesn't say a word to me or anybody else.

October 24

"My granddaddy couldn't read," Rock says. I've been telling him about Kobe in between customers, and I know he's gonna have some good advice.

"I remember him always asking me to read to him, and I didn't find out until later that it was because he couldn't."

"Whoa," I say. "I don't want that to be Kobe. He knows how to read, I guess, but he goes super slow."

"That's something to work with," Rock says. "Sounds like

the kid knows how to read, he just don't do it well. Big difference."

"But what do I do?" I ask.

"Exactly what you been doing," Rock tells me. "Be there for him."

"But I wanna help him with reading," I say. "I wanna help him the way you're helping Antwan."

Rock studies me for a second, glances over at Antwan, who's sitting in the extra barber chair. He's got earbuds in and is mumbling lyrics to himself.

"And how exactly am I 'helping' him?" Rock asks.

"I don't know." I shrug. "But you are. He's doing better, right?"

"The li'l dude you're mentoring—what's his name again?"

"Kobe," I say.

"Right. Li'l Kobe. Truth is, Isaiah, Kobe gonna have to want it. You won't be able to force him, just like I can't force Antwan to do anything."

I crack up when Rock says that, cuz he can definitely make Antwan do a lot of things.

"What? Why you laughing?" Rock asks.

"I'm just sayin'; you could tell Antwan to scrub the floor with a toothbrush and he would do it."

"Oh yeah? You think so?"

Rock claps his hands, which catches me off guard and makes

me jump. His voice rumbles like thunder when he calls to Antwan.

"Yo! Antwan!"

Antwan pulls the earbuds out and goes, "Huh?"

"Ay, man, I need you to clean this floor," Rock says. "With a toothbrush."

"What?"

"You heard me! Get to it!"

Antwan sucks his teeth and looks at the ceiling like he can't believe Rock is serious, but he stands up and studies the floor.

"A toothbrush, bro?"

"Yeah, bro, a toothbrush," Rock says. Now he can't hold back his chuckle and neither can I.

"Man, y'all play too much!" Antwan says, settling back into his chair.

"See! He was gonna do it!" I tell Rock.

"Maybe so," Rock says. "Maybe so."

"I need your superpowers!" I say.

"You still tryna save the day, huh?" Rock says, resting his hand on my head and messing with my hair. "What I tell you 'bout that?"

"I'm just doing what my dad would want me to do," I say. "He'd want me to help."

"I feel you, and I agree," Rock says. "But remember, showing up and being consistent is sometimes the best way to help. Use what you know, your own superpowers, not what you *think* you should do."

I nod, but I'm not sure what Rock is saying. That happens sometimes; he'll say some stuff that makes no sense to me, then tap a finger to the side of his head like he just gave me the answer to everything. It would take a hundred bowls of magic beans and rice to figure out all the things Rock be saying!

"Did your granddaddy ever learn to read?" I ask.

"He did," Rock says. "Went every day to the library for classes until he got it. And you wanna know the first book he checked out?"

"What?"

"A kiddie book, something about a mouse and a cookie. He got it and read it to his very first great-grandbaby."

"That's cool," I say. "If your granddaddy could do it, so can Kobe, right?"

"Absolutely!"

I like that word.

Absolutely.

October 26

If You Give a Mouse a Cookie.

That's the book Rock was talking about. I know, cuz I asked

Mr. Shephard and he knew right away which book I meant. I check out a copy and read it to Charlie for practice.

"What you think?" I ask her at the end.

"Again!" Charlie says.

I read her the book two more times before she bounces off to something else. That's gotta be a good sign. No lie, I really like the book, too, but as soon as Charlie leaves, I switch over to my favorite reading: Daddy's notebook.

I grab the blue one today because I know it's like a journal and it's always cool to see Daddy's thoughts. Like on page 24, Daddy wrote about words living forever, like stars that never go out. It's actually true, cuz Daddy isn't here but his words still are, shining brightly.

"You musta read those a thousand times in the past few months."

I look up and see Mama standing in the doorway, a small smile on her face.

"Yeah," I say. "And I'll probably read them a thousand more times."

Mama comes all the way in the room and sits next to me on my bed. She runs her fingers over the words, like she's pretending they're Daddy's hands or something.

"I'm glad you have these, Isaiah," she says. "I'm glad he left us this."

"Did Daddy know he was gonna die?" I ask, without thinking. I check Mama's face for storm clouds, but she looks strong.

"No, baby, he didn't," Mama tells me. She rubs my shoulder. "I know he'd rather be here with us, seeing you develop into this amazing writer!"

"You think so, Mama? You like my poems?"

"I love them!" Mama says. "Your words are powerful, and you're only eleven!"

"That's what Rock says, too, Mama," I say. I make my voice deep like his. " 'The pen is powerful, li'l man.' "

Mama and I laugh, cuz it's exactly how Rock sounds.

"Well, Mr. Rock is right! One day your words will inspire somebody just like Daddy's words are inspiring you," Mama says. She pulls me in for a hug, but an idea hits me and I jump up.

"Mama, that's it!" I exclaim.

"What's it?" she asks.

"My words! I know something I can do with them!"

I grab my notebook and flip to a blank page as the words start coming.

"Well, I guess I'll leave you to it, Mr. Secrets," Mama jokes.

"Okay, Mama. No offense, but I gotta get to this hero work!"

October 27

SMACK!

This time it's me slamming a folder on the table by Angel in art class. She jumps, and I can't stop the grin from sliding across my face. Then I get serious.

"We need to pause the business."

"What?"

Angel's look changes from surprised to confused to low-key angry. Yikes!

"@Dunn Poems," I say. "We need to chill with the card stuff for a minute. Check this out!"

I open the folder and grab the pack of papers that I stapled together last night—well, really early this morning—when I finished my project.

Angel scrunches up her face and picks up the papers.

"*The Bucket Chronicles of Kobe Love*?" she asks. "What is this? And who *tried* to do the art?"

"Stop hating and read it!" I say. "It's for Kobe!"

A funny noise slips from Angel's mouth, kind of a mix between a snort and a laugh. She covers her mouth but not soon enough. I just shake my head. Typical Angel, laughing before she knows the whole story.

"Yo, Ms. Marlee would be disappointed in you right now," I say, sitting beside her.

"I'm sorry, I'm sorry!" Angel says, still trying not to laugh. I mean, I get it; my drawings aren't that good. But that's where Angel comes in.

Before Mrs. Scott starts class, I tell Angel about the stories my dad wrote for me and how I'm gonna do the same thing for Kobe.

"So you gonna write him as a superhero?" Angel asks.

"Yeah, I think he'll like it."

"Bucket, though?" Angel's face is twisted up again.

I sigh and shake my head. For once, I'm the one schooling Angel.

"He's into basketball, calls himself a walking bucket," I say. "That means he hits his shots."

"I know what a walking bucket is, Isaiah," Angel says, rolling her eyes. "You forget who I live with."

"Hey, I'm just sayin'." I shrug. "You looked a little confused."

Angel glares at me, but before she makes some smart comment Mrs. Scott takes attendance and has us pick different partners for today's project. I work with this kid named Kevon and don't get to finish talking to Angel till after class.

"Aight, so it's a decent idea," she says once we're in the hallway. "But the drawings suck, so you need to just let me handle that."

"That's why I told you. @Dunn Poems can—"

"And we gotta do better than just some stapled paper!" Angel interrupts. "You can't give him some raggedy mess and expect him to like it."

"Ummm, okay?" I say. "So meet at the library this weekend?"

"Absolutely." Angel nods. She rattles off some other things

we need to do, but I'm stuck on that word. Might be my favorite word of all time.

October 30

I'm on the edge of my seat, waiting for Ms. Marlee to tell us it's free time. That's when I'm gonna give Kobe *The Bucket Chronicles of Kobe Love, Part 1*. Kobe's just as excited for free time, only he wants to head to the gym.

"Aight, let's go!" Kobe says, jumping up as soon as Ms. Marlee says the words. He reaches under his seat for his basketball.

"Hold on, I got something for you," I say, grabbing my backpack.

Kobe groans. "More baby books? C'mon, bro!"

"Nah, not baby books. *Your* book!"

I hand Kobe the book and I gotta admit, it looks tight! Angel is a craft store fanatic, and she found these blank books that look just like the real thing. I wrote the story in pencil first, to make sure I didn't mess anything up, and then I went over the words with Angel's gel pens. On the cover, Angel drew a cartoon Kobe with a glowing basketball. She drew little basketballs and nets on the pages, too. Kobe's eyes get wide when he sees it.

"That supposed to be me?" he asks.

"Nah, it's just this kid superhero named Kobe Love," I say. "Saves people using his magic basketball."

Kobe stares at the cover, and I think he's reading the words. After a few seconds he points at one of them.

"What's that word?" he asks.

"Chronicles," I say.

"And what's that mean?"

"It's like, a collection of stories."

"How did the basketball get to be magic?"

"He found it in the Garden of Orange Legends."

"What's that?"

"You never heard of that?" I say. "It's the final resting place of all the basketball greats, kinda like a magical graveyard. They call it GOOL for short."

"So what does he do with the ball?" asks Kobe.

"You gotta read it for yourself," I tell him. "How 'bout we read a few pages, and then go hoop."

"Aight," Kobe agrees. We turn to the first page and I read it out loud.

In the city of Spalding,
where the best ballers play,
A kid named Kobe Love
Had a really bad day.

I read about how superhero Kobe got in trouble at school, and instead of getting off the city bus at his stop, he just rode and rode until he fell asleep. When he woke up, he was at the entrance of GOOL.

The bus driver turned, with a grin on his face.
"You're in luck, li'l man, this a real special place.
Take your time, look around, but beware after
*   dark.*
I'll drive around twice, but I can't stop and park."

I keep thinking Kobe's gonna interrupt me and say he's ready to play ball, but he doesn't. We finish the story, which ends with superhero Kobe missing the bus and being stuck at GOOL after dark. That's when he finds the magic basketball.

"Yo, what happens next?" Kobe asks when I close the book. "What's he gonna do with the ball?"

"This is only Part One," I say. "We'll read Part Two next week."

"Aight," Kobe says. He actually takes the book and puts it in his bag. Then he grabs his ball and tosses it up and down.

"If I had a magic ball, I'd fix everything!" he says.

"Yeah? Like what?"

Kobe's quiet for a second.

"Everything," he says. "Ready to play?"

"Yeah, let's go."

Angel gives me a thumbs-up as me and Kobe head to the gym. Not gonna lie, there's no Part 2 yet, but words are already swirling around in my head, excited to come out.

November 2

For the first time in a while, I feel really good about what @Dunn Poems is doing. I mean, we're making *real* books. Kinda. I figure we can put out a new *Bucket Chronicles* every week, which means I have to come up with a lot of ideas. To be honest, I use some of Daddy's story ideas, like when superhero

Isaiah Dunn had to play in a championship basketball game. For Part 2, I change that up a little, and it's superhero Kobe Love on a basketball court with bullies. The magic basketball helps him and some younger kids win a pickup game.

"So *every* story gotta be about basketball?" Angel asks.

I took the day off from the barbershop, and me and Angel are at the library, crunching on leftover Halloween candy, and she's reading the next story in my notebook. We have this strategy where I have the story written by Thursday, and then Angel works on the drawings until Sunday so Kobe can get his book on Monday.

"It's a magic basketball, Angel," I say, like *duh*! "Plus, he really likes basketball. I gotta have it in the books."

"I guess," Angel says, but she doesn't look convinced. "I'm just sayin', I don't wanna be drawing only basketballs all the time."

"So, be creative!" I say. Obviously the glowing ball has to be in each story, but there's a lot of other stuff that Angel can draw. I start writing her a list while she keeps reading.

"The poems are nice, but we gotta talk about something," Angel says, closing the notebook.

Uh-oh.

"What?"

"We ain't makin' no money," Angel says. "I mean, *you* probably are since you have a whole other business. But *we* aren't."

She's right. And wrong. Right because we haven't done

anything with her greeting card idea or her invitation idea, and we haven't done POTS—Poems on the Spot—in a while, either. I feel kinda bad that Angel's ideas were moneymakers and mine isn't, but everything about the *Bucket Chronicles* just feels right.

But Angel's wrong if she thinks I'm making tons of money with Sneaky's candy business. He's been more into football lately, and he said kids won't really be buying candy this soon after Halloween.

"We're not making a lot right now, but we will," I tell Angel. "And I have money saved up so you don't have to pay for the books."

Angel sighs, and she looks just like Sneaky would if I said we needed to give candy away for free.

"How long you wanna do these books?" Angel asks.

"I don't know," I say. "As long as I need to, especially if it helps Kobe. I gotta be a good mentor, remember?" I grin and use Angel's words, so she really can't get mad.

"Ugh!" she says. "Guess I'm gonna have to work with my dad. He said I could help with team stuff once it's basketball season."

"What's wrong with that?" I ask.

"Ummm, my dad gets pretty intense when it comes to sports," Angel says.

"It's cuz he loves it," I say. I tell Angel what Rock said about Now and Later dreams. Coaching is probably her dad's Now dream.

"I think it's his Later dream, too," Angel says. "I mean, he likes his job driving the city bus and everything, but he really wants to be a college coach, maybe even the NFL. When we were in Atlanta, my uncles and aunts told him to stop talking about it and be about it."

"Wow, your family sounds just like you," I say.

Angel smacks my arm. "I think he's gonna go for it," she says. "I just hope he don't coach at the college I go to!"

"Nah, I think it would be cool to have my dad around at my school," I say.

"Oh. Sorry."

Angel's quiet for a second and I know she's probably thinking about my dad being gone. Angel once said that when her dad got laid off last year, he changed a lot and would yell at everyone all the time because of the stress. I guess it was kinda like how Mama was after Daddy died. For Angel's dad, a new job and coaching is what helped him. For Mama, I guess it's Miz Rita and doing her school stuff. And for me, it's definitely these books.

"So anyway, about the business," I say, changing the subject so Angel doesn't feel sorry for me. "How 'bout we just focus on *Bucket Chronicles* for now?"

"Why can't we do both?"

I decide to just tell Angel the truth.

"I'm kinda tired of doing the cards," I say. "I mean, they're cool and all, but I like doing the *Chronicles* more."

I hold my breath, waiting for Angel to explode.

"Wowwww," Angel says. "So you tired of having the business?"

"Nah, I just think . . . we need to look at the identity of the business."

"Isaiah." Angel stares at me and blinks super slow.

"Huh?"

"You doing the most right now."

"It's how I feel, though," I say.

"Yeah? Well, I feel like we should be making money!" Angel says.

"We will!"

"When?"

"I don't know!"

Mr. Shephard walks by and taps our table.

"Must be some great ideas churning over here," he says. "Just make sure you keep the excitement down, alright?"

I nod. Angel glares.

"You mad?" I ask after a few minutes of us not talking.

Angel sighs extra loud.

"No," she says. "But business partners are supposed to make decisions together."

"Okay, so how about this," I say. "We keep doing Poems on the Spot, but we also work on the *Bucket Chronicles*."

"That works, I guess," Angel says after thinking about it. "It's getting cold outside so we can go to the mall for Poems on the Spot. And we HAVE to do Christmas cards! Do you know how much money people spend on those?"

"See? You sounding like Sneaky again," I say, shaking my head.

"Ewww, no I do not!"

"Whatever. So are we good?" I ask Angel.

"For now," Angel says with a smirk. She gathers her pens to start drawing.

Whew! Being a double business partner is way harder than I thought!

November 6

"Where's the next one?"

It's the first thing out of Kobe's mouth after we read *Bucket Chronicles* Part 2, even before he grabs his ball to go to the gym. He hasn't read out loud yet, but like Ms. Marlee says, baby steps grow if you keep taking them.

"Next week, bro," I say.

"Maaannn, this is like waiting for TV show episodes!" Kobe groans. "Can you bring two next time?"

"Maybe," I say.

I grin at Angel as me and Kobe head to the gym. She and

her mentee, Zani, are coloring this giant page of desserts, and it looks pretty good. Kobe is running his mouth and dribbling as we walk down the hall, and we both turn when we hear voices behind us. When Kobe sees who it is, the ball bounces off his foot—which *never* happens—and rolls against the lockers.

Matthew and Tony.

Kobe's face gets hard, and he snatches up the ball. Now he's pounding it into the ground as he dribbles, and the echo is super loud in the hall.

"You good?" I ask when we get to the gym.

Kobe nods and launches up a shot that banks in off the backboard.

"I will be if people keep my name out their mouth," he says loudly.

Me and Kobe shoot on one end of the court, and Matthew and Tony stay on the other end. All good.

"How's school going?" I ask. It's our routine now; we pass the ball and ask a question. The other person answers the question and takes a shot. If you make your shot, you get to ask the next question. If you miss, the other person keeps asking questions until you make it. Not gonna lie, I think both of us are getting better at making shots.

"Good."

Swish!

"How's your girlfriend doing?" Kobe asks.

I shake my head. I know he's talking about Angel.

"I don't have a girlfriend," I say, taking my shot. I miss. Kobe laughs.

"You sure 'bout that?"

"Yes." I make my shot and ask Kobe another question.

"You get in trouble last week?"

"Nope!" Kobe makes a layup. "Did you?"

"Nope," I say, but I miss my shot again. Kobe shakes his head.

"But you used to, right? Ms. Marlee said all the mentors had to go through Rocket ReStore."

"Yeah, I did," I say. My shot rims around before falling in. I tell him that me and Angel used to fight, but that we're friends now.

"You fought your girlfriend? Wowww, bro!" Kobe says. "And y'all turned into friends?"

"Yup," I say. "Think that can happen with you and Tony?"

Kobe doesn't shoot, just gives me a look like, *No way!*

"Nah, we ain't never gonna be friends," Kobe says. "He do too much! Always talking about people and stuff."

"That's how Angel was," I say, trying a layup. This is what usually happens. After a few questions, we stop keeping track and just shoot and talk.

"That's cool for you, but not me," Kobe says.

"He teases you a lot?" I ask.

"Yeah," Kobe says.

"Cuz of the reading stuff?"

"Yo, can we just play ball?" Kobe says.

"Yeah," I say. "You know how to play Elephant?"

"Elephant?" Kobe wrinkles his nose.

I explain how it's like Horse but better, and we start shooting. I'm on the second "e" and Kobe's on the first "e" when Matthew and Tony wander over.

"Hey, y'all wanna play two-on-two?" Matthew asks.

"Y'all wanna get beat?" Kobe asks, mean-mugging Tony.

"Kobe, chill," I say.

"Yeah, chill," Tony echoes with a smirk. Matthew elbows him.

"We only got a few minutes left if you wanna play," Matthew says.

I look at Kobe, and he gives me a nod.

"First to ten," he says, then leans closer to me. "Yo, it's just like in the story! We gotta bring that bully down!"

Matthew and Tony take the ball out first, and Kobe immediately steals it and passes to me. I fake a shot and pass back to him. *Swish!* The game moves fast after that. Matthew hits a few shots and Tony does, too. I'm watching the game as much as I'm playing, and even though Tony's taller, Kobe is definitely better. He barely misses a shot, even when Tony's hands are all in his face. We're up 8–5 when Ms. Marlee comes into the gym to tell us that time is up. Even though the game is over and Matthew and Tony start walking toward the door, Kobe still fires up two more shots. Swish and swish, nine and ten.

"Yo, Isaiah," he says, staring at the basketball. "Don't laugh or nothing, but I think this ball might really be magic."

I don't laugh, but I do grin.

"Nah, it's just a ball. I think *you* got the magic."

"Yeah." Kobe dribbles a few times. "You already know! It's always magic when it's in my hands!"

November 8

Kobe might have the basketball magic, but I am definitely missing the money magic. I count my stash of money a third time, but the number doesn't change.

I gave Angel money for eight more blank books since her mom is taking her to the craft store today. Not gonna lie, it kinda hurts to see the money leaving and not coming back in. Daddy's sock, where I keep my money, is looking real empty right now. I sigh and put the sock back under my bed. I used to keep it in my backpack, but when it got stolen I had to find a safer spot.

I get out my notebook and start the next *Bucket Chronicles* story, which I decide is gonna be about superhero Kobe helping his best friend find some money he lost. Writing best friend poems makes me think about Sneaky. We haven't hung out in a while and I wonder if he's home or at football practice. Only one way to find out.

I barely finish knocking when the door flies open, and Sneaky's standing there with a grin on his face.

"Yo, Isaiah, I was just about to come down to your place!" he says, giving me dap.

"I know," I say, tapping the side of my head the way Rock does. "Best friends always know these things."

"Oh yeah?" Sneaky says. "Bet you don't know what I been workin' on!"

I follow Sneaky to the kitchen where it's pretty much a hot mess. There's candy wrappers, half-empty ice-cream cartons, and banana peels all over the place, and whatever's in Sneaky's blender is also splattered on the counter. Sneaky hands me a cup.

"Bro, taste this!"

I peek in the cup first, and whatever it is looks thick and beige with brown and red specks.

"Just try it!"

I take a sip. Then another. It's actually . . . good.

"What is this?" I ask.

"You like it, right? I was gonna drink one of Wes's work-out shake thingies cuz I'm trying to put on some muscle, and it was straight nasty! So I turned it into a milkshake. Kinda. But better."

I look around the kitchen and see the empty bottles on the counter.

"Yo, is Wes gonna be mad that you're drinking his stuff?" I ask.

Sneaky shrugs. "If he's smart, he'll appreciate the upgrade," he says, taking a sip from his own cup. "I should be, like, a chef or something."

"Yeah, have your own shake restaurant," I say. "And shakes for athletes. I bet they pay a lot for stuff like that."

"Oh, you right!" Sneaky says. His eyes get real wide. " 'Saiah, guess what we can call it?"

"Sneaky's Shakes?"

"Nah, bro, the Candy Boy Shake!"

"That's fire!"

"I'm a genius!" Sneaky yells, pumping his fist.

"We got the best drink you could ever make. Get your dollars out and try the Candy Boy Shake!" I say. Sneaky goes wild and we do our dance. We're adding a new part when the apartment door opens and Sneaky's mom comes into the kitchen a few seconds later. Yikes!

"Ma, don't even worry about this," Sneaky says quickly. "Me and 'Saiah 'bout to clean it up, but yo, lemme pour you something to drink."

Sneaky scrambles to pour his mom a cup while she fusses at him about the mess. All it takes is one sip, though, and she quiets down.

"You like it?" Sneaky asks.

"I like my kitchen clean," his mom snaps. "I'm gonna go watch my show, and it betta be clean in here by the time I'm done!"

Sneaky's all grins as his mom heads to the living room. Even though my money is mad low and I'm stuck helping clean up this mess, I'm all grins, too.

November 16

Today should be just a regular, normal Thursday. But it's not. It's a week before Thanksgiving, and everybody's talking about where they're gonna go and what they're gonna eat.

"Bro, I can't wait for my granny's mac 'n' cheese," Sneaky says at lunch. Him, his mom, and Antwan always go visit their grandma in Chicago for Thanksgiving. Angel and her family are going to Atlanta, and Kobe's staying at home. He said his dad isn't coming home for Thanksgiving, but he'll be here for Christmas.

Thanksgiving ain't a bad holiday. I used to like it a lot. But now, all I think about is last year and how Daddy died on that day.

I think Mama is feeling it, too, cuz when I get home from school, she gives me a big hug and holds on for a little longer than normal. Her eyes look sad, so I don't say anything about Daddy; I just tell her how I got 93% on my social studies quiz.

"That's what I'm talkin' about!" Mama says. She reaches in her bag and pulls out a paper she had to write for her school. Ninety-one out of one hundred, right at the top.

"See? You even got your moms beat!" she says.

When I go into the kitchen for some juice, I see a bunch of Charlie's drawings on the refrigerator. Most of them are of Superdog, but she has other pictures, too. The latest one is of me, Charlie, Mama, Daddy, Miz Rita, and a dog. I never thought of Charlie missing Daddy the way I do, but I guess she does. She doesn't talk about him that much, but she still draws him in family pictures.

"All this doesn't bother you, Miz Rita?" I ask. I know I would get tired of seeing ponies and rainbows and stick figures on my refrigerator, especially if I didn't have kids.

"Absolutely not! These are masterpieces," Miz Rita says, using my favorite word. "You got something you want me to put up there?"

"I dunno," I say. "I'm too old for all that."

"Oh really? How 'bout one of your famous poems, then?"

"Yeah, I could write a poem," I tell Miz Rita. "I'll write one about the good food you be cooking!"

Miz Rita laughs.

"I'll make sure to save a spot for that one!" she says.

I sip my grape juice and watch Miz Rita slide a pan of cornbread into the oven.

"Miz Rita," I say.

"Yes, baby?"

I stare at my socks for a second, nervous about what I want to say to her. It's only because I overheard her on the phone last night, telling one of her friends she couldn't make it to some meeting because she'd be watching Charlie while Mama was at school.

"I can watch Charlie, you know. While Mama's in class, I mean."

"I'm sure you can," Miz Rita says, peeking into the pot on the stove. "But that's not necessary right now."

"You not tired of us staying here?"

Miz Rita puts down the spoon she was using for the chili and turns to face me with her hand on her hip.

"Isaiah Dunn! I know you did not just ask me that!" Miz Rita says. "Have I told you I was tired of having you here?"

"No," I mumble, still staring at the ground.

"Well, I haven't said that because I'm not tired," says Miz Rita. "You, your mama, and Charlie baby are welcome here for as long as you need. I guess you don't know that y'all are a blessing to me. Yessir, a just-in-time blessing!"

Miz Rita says that since Shayna's away at college, she'd be lonely in the apartment by herself.

"Y'all bring life to this place," she says. "So no more questions like that, alright?"

"Yes, ma'am," I say.

I help Miz Rita set the table, and she hums the whole time. Daddy used to hum, too. He said it's what happens when you got so much happiness inside you but you can't let it out all at once. Miz Rita humming a lot must mean she's happy. Must mean she's telling the truth about wanting us here.

November 21

"You wrong for this, Rock," I groan, slumping down in the barber chair.

"Relax, li'l man," Rock says with a laugh. "You trust us, right?"

"Yeah, I trust *you* . . . ," I say, letting my voice trail off.

"What you sayin'? You don't trust me?" Antwan asks. He leans over to look me in the face. I shrug.

"I mean . . ."

I don't really know how to tell Antwan that nah, I really don't trust him cutting my hair. Rock starts talking, trying to calm me down.

"Listen, li'l man, we gonna change it up a bit. When this is all said and done, you gonna have a nice bald fade, alright?"

"And if I mess up, it's just gonna be bald!" Antwan says with a pretty sinister laugh.

"Yo, that ain't funny!" I say, almost jumping out the chair.

"Chill, I got you," Antwan says.

"And I'm standing right here," Rock adds.

I squeeze my eyes shut and start praying. I used to get buzz cuts when I was little and maaan, it was not a good look, no matter how cute Mama says it was. Even Daddy said I'm the type of guy who needs some hair on his head. I don't wanna be bald!

Please, God! Please, God!

I feel Antwan pull the comb through my hair and hear the clippers buzz on.

Rock talks to Antwan, telling him how to hold the clippers and use them to fade the sides of my head.

"Look, see how his hair grows right there? Cut just like this, okay?"

Rock takes the clippers and, for a second, I can breathe again. Rock swipes my hair with the clippers a few times, then hands them back to Antwan.

Please, God! Please, God!

"We gonna leave some hair at the top, so go ahead and switch guards," Rock tells Antwan. He taps a spot on the right side of my head. "See this right here? We gotta blend that up real good."

Antwan runs the clippers back and forth, and I'm gripping the arms of the barber chair for dear life.

"Relax, 'Saiah, you alright!" Antwan tells me. "I'm not gonna mess you up."

He's sayin' that, but I can't stop picturing him making one

wrong swipe and giving me a bald spot. Daddy did that once, only cuz he was watching a Pistons game and they kept turning the ball over. Daddy said the bald spot wasn't that bad. It was.

"That's good, Antwan," Rock says. "See how that blends real nice? You got it, man!"

Antwan does some more combing and cutting, then Rock edges me up just as a *real* customer (not a guinea pig) comes in.

"Time for the fire!" Rock says, spraying alcohol on my head and handing me a mirror.

"Open your eyes, bro," Antwan says, smacking my arm. "Quit playin'!"

I peek with one eye, then both.

Whoa.

My haircut ain't a disaster! I turn my head from side to side and check out the back. No bald spots, no messed-up hairline.

Antwan's over there grinning and giving me a look like, *Uh-huh, say somethin'!*

"Whatchoo think?" Rock asks, handing me a broom. Yeah, he makin' me sweep up after my own haircut!

"It's aight," I say.

"Bro!"

"Okay, okay, it's actually good, Antwan," I say. "Thanks."

"Don't y'all ever forget the power you got in your hands," Rock tells us, holding up his. "Clippers or the pen, they're both powerful when you use them the right way."

I stare at my hands, imagining that they're my superpower. They sure feel lucky when Rock puts a ten-dollar bill in them!

In the car, Mama tells me how good my haircut looks.

"Rock done gave me my baby back!"

"Mama, come on!"

"Hey, I'm just sayin'," Mama laughs.

"And it wasn't even Rock who did this," I tell her. "Antwan did."

"What?! He can cut that good?"

"Well, Rock helped him, but only a little."

"Wow." Mama keeps glancing from the road to my hair. "Good for him."

We ride in silence for a while, and then Mama takes a deep breath.

"'Saiah, I've been thinking about something," she says.

I turn to face her. We been having so many good days, but the way Mama's looking right now, my stomach starts karate-chopping and I wonder if bad days are coming back.

"What is it, Mama?" I ask when she doesn't say anything right away.

"I been thinking, I want to do something different this year," Mama says slowly. "For Thanksgiving."

When she says that word—*Thanksgiving*—my chest tightens up. I can't help but think about last year. Mama started cooking the night before, like she always does. Me and Charlie woke up early to the sound of pots and pans being moved around and '90s R&B music blasting on Daddy's Bluetooth speaker. It smelled sooo good in our apartment! Daddy made his famous greens, and Mama always said they had a kick at the end of them. Mama made banana pudding and sweet potato pie and a caramel cake with thick frosting that me and Charlie kept swiping when Mama wasn't looking. Turkey, mac 'n' cheese, dressing, sweet rolls from scratch, all the good stuff.

We didn't even get to eat that dinner.

"I want us to get away—a quick vacation," Mama says.

"With Miz Rita?" I ask.

"No, just the three of us," Mama says. "Just us."

I stare out my window and think about it for a second. Maybe getting away would be a good thing. I know we'll still be thinking about Daddy, but at least we won't have to be in the same building where we were last year. Or anywhere around the parade.

Sometimes I think that maybe if we hadn't gone to the Thanksgiving parade, Daddy would still be here. We could've just chilled at home, watched the football game, and smashed all that good food. But nah. We had to go downtown. Mama had said it was spontaneous, and Charlie was repeating that word the whole car ride there. *Spontaneous.*

"That would be cool, I guess," I tell Mama. Honestly, whatever we gotta do to get through that day is what we gotta do.

November 23

"Stop splashing me, Isaiah!"

"You splashed me!" I yell, sending more water her way. Charlie covers her face and squeals, but she's loving this. Mama, too.

I still can't believe we're here! Lazy Lakes for three whole days! It's kinda far away, so both me and Charlie fell asleep on the drive. We woke up super quick when Mama announced where we were, though!

We're at the wave pool now and every time the bell rings, the waves get real big. I leave Mama and Charlie in the shallow part and go out where the waves are really choppy. If you relax and stay still, the waves move you around, and it almost feels like being a baby and getting rocked. When the waves stop, I splash Charlie some more.

"'Saiah, can you watch Charlie for a second?" Mama asks when the waves start back up. "I wanna try that."

"You gonna ride the waves, Mama?" I ask, taking Charlie's hand.

"Something like that," she says.

Mama moves toward the deep end and at first she's fighting to stay on her feet.

"Just float, Mama!" I yell. I don't think she hears me, though, cuz everybody's screaming and laughing and splashing. I pretend I'm Isaiah Dunn, Superhero, and that my words can instantly zoom to Mama even though we're far apart. It seems like it works! When I look over at Mama again, she's stretched out, just letting the waves rock her.

"Mama's having fun!" Charlie says, jumping on my back.

I take her out a little deeper until her fingers are digging in my chest cuz she doesn't wanna fall off.

"Owww! I got you, Charlie; just relax!" I say.

"Don't drop me, 'Saiah!"

"I won't!"

I let Charlie get rocked by the waves for what feels like forever, while Mama stays in the deep end floating. Our fingers and toes are like raisins by the time we finally get out! I don't know about Mama and Charlie, but I completely forget that it's Thanksgiving . . . until we're at dinner.

We eat at this restaurant in the resort called the Sandcastle, and there's a special Thanksgiving menu with turkey, stuffing, mashed potatoes, rolls, and green beans. Mama stares at that menu for a long time. Bet she's thinking about how much better her and Daddy's food is. Maybe she's missing his greens. I know I am. We been having a real good time, and I hope this menu doesn't mess everything up.

"I want pizza!" Charlie says loudly. "And French fries and broccoli and pineapples!"

"Charlie!" I say through gritted teeth, glancing at Mama.

Mama looks up with a smile, though, and pushes the Thanksgiving menu away.

"Now that you said something, Charlie, pizza sounds amazing!" Mama says.

And that's what we order. One extra-large pizza with onions and peppers on Mama's side, and just cheese on me and Charlie's. We get fries and broccoli, too, but the restaurant has apple slices instead of pineapple. We're all okay with that. For dessert, me and Charlie get ice-cream sundaes and Mama gets a slice of pecan pie, which is one of her favorites.

Pretty soon, we're all yawning and ready to head to our room, which is super nice. Mama has her own giant bed, and me and Charlie have bunk beds in this cave-like area of the room. Last night, Charlie was scared to sleep on the bottom, so we switched. Then she was scared at the top, so we switched again! I wonder where she'll be tonight.

Before we go to sleep, Mama asks what we're thankful for, and Charlie says she's thankful for the Screaming Rapids slide that we got on.

"I'm thankful that Isaiah held my arm like this"—Charlie demonstrates to Mama—"cuz I almost fell off!"

"I'm glad he held on to you, too!" Mama says. "I bet that was scary!"

"Nah." Charlie shrugs. "We're getting on it again tomorrow, right, 'Saiah?"

"I guess," I say, remembering how much convincing it took to get Charlie on the slide in the first place.

"What about you, Isaiah?" Mama asks. "What are you thankful for?"

I take only a second to think.

"I'm thankful for you, Mama," I say.

"What about me?" pouts Charlie.

"And you, Charlie. I was gonna say that."

Daddy's notebook is sitting in my lap, and even though it's kind of a sad day, I have to say something else.

"I'm also thankful for Daddy's words," I say. "They make me feel close to him, like he's still here talking. I'm thankful he wrote so much."

Mama nods and squeezes my hand.

"Mama, lay down and listen to 'Saiah read, okay?" Charlie says. Mama cuddles up with Charlie, and they both wait for me to begin.

"*The Beans and Rice Chronicles of Isaiah Dunn,* story number one," I say.

Maybe it's because we spent so much time in the water today, or maybe because we stuffed ourselves on pizza and ice cream . . . It could be that the bunk bed is super comfy, or that my reading voice is *absolutely* spectacular . . . It's probably all those things put together that make Mama and Charlie fall asleep before Isaiah Dunn, Superhero, even finishes a bowl of beans and rice.

November 27

"So how was it, bro? You guys good?"

"Yeah, we're good," I say. "Lazy Lakes was awesome."

"That's cool," Sneaky says. "My mom was worried about y'all the whole break. She kept sayin' 'Lord, I hope Lisa and them babies are alright.'"

Sneaky imitates his mom, which is always hilarious. It's good to know she was thinking about us. Sneaky's mom invited us to spend Thanksgiving with them, and I think Mama almost said yes. Miz Rita wanted us to spend Thanksgiving with her and Shayna and some people from her church. She said they were renting a spot and that it would be good for us to be with people who care about us. Mama almost said yes to that, too, but I'm glad she stuck to our spontaneous plan.

"I'm gonna ask to go there for my birthday," Sneaky says.

"Yeah, okay." I laugh. I doubt his mom is gonna do all that, but who knows!

When school's over, I walk under the covered walkway to Woodson Elementary, which is right next to the middle school. Kobe's already there, dribbling his basketball in Ms. Marlee's room and telling her about his Thanksgiving.

"Yo, Isaiah, I ate so much turkey I think I grew a few inches!" Kobe tells me. He's dead serious, too!

"What you do for break?" he asks me.

"Stayed in the water," I say. "We went to Lazy Lakes."

"For real?" Kobe's eyes get wide. "Y'all must be rich! I'ma be rich, too, when I get in the NBA, and I'ma *buy* Lazy Lakes!"

"Well, I'll for sure visit when you do!" Ms. Marlee says.

"I'ma remember you, Ms. Marlee," Kobe says. "You too, Isaiah."

"You betta!" I say.

In today's meeting, Ms. Marlee talks about self-control and how it's important for school and life.

"Yeah, I don't have none of that," Kobe whispers while she talks. I chuckle cuz he's right. He told me his teacher called him a live wire, and his granny says he's got a wild streak in him. I think about how mad I got when Angel was messing with me—mad enough to push her out her chair! When Ms. Marlee tells us to break off in pairs and talk to each other about a time when we had no self-control, I tell Kobe that story.

"I'm just sayin'; she deserved that!" Kobe tells me.

"Maybe," I say. "But I got suspended and my mom was real mad, so it wasn't a good choice."

"Well, you already know mine," Kobe says, glaring across the room at Tony. "He deserved what he got, too!"

"It got you in trouble, though," I say.

"So?" Kobe acts like it's no big deal, but he's looking at his shoes, so I know he doesn't like the getting in trouble part.

"So, wasn't it better to beat him on the court?" I ask, thinking back to our game. Once Kobe started raining shots, Tony didn't have much to say.

"He wasn't ready for me," Kobe says with a smirk.

"Hey, you can always try the breathing thing if he makes you mad again," I say. Ms. Marlee always starts our meetings with different breathing exercises, and to be honest, they do help me calm down.

"Breathing?" Kobe makes a face.

"Yeah, you gotta try different things to see what works," I tell him.

Kobe exaggerates the breathing exercise we did today, and it makes me laugh.

"Yo, if that works for you, do it!" I say.

"I won't even need it," Kobe says. "I'm doing good now. Teacher hasn't called my granny or my mom all week!"

"It's Monday, Kobe," I say, shaking my head.

"See! One day at a time, like y'all always say!"

When we get to our free time, Kobe reaches in his bag and pulls out a book—I'm shocked!

"I read this over break. I like how the words be rhyming. My granny does, too," he tells me, holding up *Bucket Chronicles* Part 4. It's when Superhero Kobe goes back to the GOOL to try and talk to his favorite basketball player.

"That's what's up," I say, giving him dap.

"You got the next one?" Kobe asks.

"Yup!" I say.

Kobe asks if we can read in the gym, and when we get there he tosses me his basketball.

"Every sentence I read, you gotta take a shot from back here, okay?"

"Bet," I say.

Kobe reads slowly, so I don't have to take a bunch of shots, but he's excited when I hit a few and I'm excited that he's reading.

When Mama and Charlie pick me up after Rockets Reach Back, Charlie's yelling my name as soon as I climb into the car.

"'Saiah, look what happened at school!"

I turn around to see Charlie grinning big, only she's missing something . . . two teeth! They've been wiggly for a while, and I guess they finally came out.

"Whoa, Charlie, look at all that space!" I say.

"It feels funny!" Charlie says, running her teeth over her front gums.

"It *looks* funny!" I laugh. Mama swats my arm, but she's laughing, too.

"Stop it! She's cute!"

"I guess," I say with a shrug.

"I was playing catch like you showed me, but I missed the ball," Charlie says.

"Ouch! Did it hurt?"

"Nope, I was brave!" Charlie gives another gummy grin. "Superdog helped me!"

Charlie leans forward to shove a piece of paper my way, and I'm not surprised to see a toothless Superdog.

"Nice," I say. She's really into this Superdog thing. When we get to Miz Rita's, I ask Mama about it.

"Mama, you think it's weird for Charlie to be drawing Superdog all the time?"

"About as weird as your daddy writing a kid superhero who eats beans and rice for magic powers," Mama says, giving me a look.

"Oh. Guess you got a point," I say.

"To be honest," Mama says, "I think she's trying to stay connected to him, just like you."

"By drawing a dog?"

"Not just any dog . . . Superdog!" Mama says. I groan, but then I get an idea.

"Okay, Mama, so how 'bout a real dog?" I ask.

"Welllll, I think I like him better on the page," Mama says.

"But, Mama, Superdog wants to get off the page and come to our house!"

Charlie bounces into the room and overhears us.

"Is it cuz we live with Miz Rita?" I ask.

"It's . . . cuz of a lot of things," Mama says.

"Like what? I promise I'll walk him!" Charlie says, making pray-hands. "Please please please!"

"We'll see," Mama says, which is usually her nice way of saying no. Charlie don't know that, though, so she claps her hands.

"Isaiah, why don't you help your sister get washed up. I'm making grilled cheese tonight!"

I think grilled cheese is Mama's favorite sandwich, and she pretends that it's ours so she can make it a lot. When I go into Mama and Charlie's room, Charlie's staring at her teeth—or lack of teeth—in the mirror.

"Do I look bad?" she asks me. Trick question!

"Ummm, no, not really. And plus, your big teeth will grow in before you know it," I tell her.

"You gonna put some money under my pillow? Nia said she got ten dollars!"

"For a tooth? Dang!" I say.

"Well, you don't have to do that much," Charlie says, putting on her sad face. "I just don't want you guys to forget. I told Nia that Superdog was gonna put money under my pillow."

"So ask Superdog then!"

"Isaiah, you're being mean." Charlie cuts her eyes at me and goes back to the mirror.

"Relax, Charlie," I say, patting her shoulder. "You're gonna have some amazing things under your pillow when you wake up. Way better than Nia's ten bucks."

"Promise?" Charlie's eyes get all huge and excited.

"Promise," I say. She'll get some money, of course, but she'll also get the best "lost teeth" poem ever!

December 2

"So your dad named you after Isiah Thomas, and my dad named me after Kobe Bryant. Ain't that cool?"

Me and Kobe are on our way to the YMCA, but not to shoot around. He plays in this league for little kids and begged me to come to his first game. We're riding with his grandma; I found out that's who him and his mom live with since his dad is overseas.

"Yeah, it's real cool," I say.

"So you into basketball, too?" asks Kobe's grandma.

"No," I say. "I'm a writer."

"He's gonna be, though," Kobe says loudly. "It's part of this deal we made."

I give Kobe a look like, *What deal?* We're both in the backseat, and Kobe's grandma looks at us in the rearview mirror.

"Oh, a deal, huh?" says his grandma.

"Yup." Kobe grins. "'Saiah makes me do all this reading stuff, and I help him with his free throws. He's almost good enough to try out for a team."

"I'm not trying out for a team," I tell Kobe.

"Oh yeah? Even if I do this?"

Kobe reaches into his gym bag and pulls out *Bucket Chronicles* Part 5. He turns to where we left off in Rockets Reach Back and starts reading. It takes him a while to get through the sentences, but I'm smiling big when he does.

"Yo, that was real good, Kobe!" I say, holding out my fist. He pounds it hard and has a huge grin of his own. His grandma's smiling, too, from the front seat.

When we get to the Y, me and Kobe's grandma find seats on the bleachers near each other, and I'm realizing it's kinda awkward with just the two of us. I shoulda asked Sneaky to come, too.

"You know he practiced those pages all morning," Kobe's grandma says. "He wanted to impress you."

"For real?" I ask, watching Kobe warm up. He's completely different on the court, not clowning around or joking or messing with other people. He's focused.

"I always gotta get on him about his schoolwork, but never with this," his grandma says, waving her hand around the gym. "He'd be here for hours if they let him!"

"That's like me and writing, I guess," I say.

"Mmmm-hmmm, he told me you're always writing in a notebook; that's real nice," she says. "And thank you for working with Kobe, Isaiah. He really likes you; runs his mouth about you all the time. 'Isaiah this and Isaiah that.' We've had a rough few months, but we really appreciate you."

"Thanks," I say. I still can't believe Kobe likes the books and that he's actually reading them. Now I just gotta make sure the story ideas keep coming. If they did for Daddy, I know they will for me.

Right before the game starts, Kobe's grandma hands me a pack of Life Savers.

"Since you got so much in common with this candy," she says with a wink.

The Life Savers make me think about a bunch of words, so I take out my notebook and write them all down.

LIFESAVERS

Lifesavers, all colors.
Grandmas, cousins, sisters, brothers.
A hero can be anyone,
Even me, Isaiah Dunn.
A hero means you listen,
A hero means you care.
A hero isn't selfish,
And they're not afraid to share.
A hero can do little things
To make somebody big.
A hero gives it all they got
To help somebody live.
My daddy was a hero
Cuz his words help save the day.
And now it's up to me,
A lifesaver on the way!

Kobe's short and all, but man! He's a giant on the court! His team is in blue, and the red team they're playing seems shocked that he's so good. Kobe probably always gets teased about being small, and that could be why he acts how he acts. It could also be why he works so hard at being good on the court.

On this one play, when Kobe's going for a layup, a kid who's way taller runs into him and it kinda looks like a push. Kobe hits the ground and bounces up with balled fists. His grandma goes, "Aww Lawd," like she knows he's gonna explode.

But he doesn't.

The ref blows his whistle, and Kobe walks off to the side for a minute. His back is to us, but I see exactly what's going on.

"What's he doin'?" Kobe's grandma says to herself. I grin as I tell her the answer, and I can't wait to tell Ms. Marlee, too.

"He's breathing," I say.

December 7

"Yo, why it gotta be so cold outside?" Antwan complains, stomping his feet to get the snow off. Rock has him shoveling the sidewalk outside the shop, and I'm super glad I'm inside sweeping the hair-snow.

"What's funny is how you actin' so surprised about it!" Rock says with a laugh. "And I hate to break it to you, but they predicting a cold winter."

"Watch, I'm moving to Florida," Antwan says. "Yo, Rock, you should let me open up a New Growth shop down there."

"Sounds like a Later dream, Antwan," Rock tells him. "And that's good, cuz believe me on this, y'all two gonna do way bigger things than I ever did. Both of you."

Rock starts rambling about how we gotta do good in school and stay out of trouble. Antwan rolls his eyes, but I know he's listening. I am, too.

"Y'all got people looking up to you," Rock says. "Antwan, you got your hustlin' li'l brother, and, 'Saiah, you got your baby sister *and* that Kobe kid. They watching every move you make, good and bad. When you stand tall, everybody stands tall."

Two guys come in for haircuts, and Rock keeps right on talking about dreams and hard work and believing in yourself. After they both leave, Rock flips his "Open" sign to "Closed," and for a second, I think he's gonna have Antwan cut my hair again. But he doesn't.

"Y'all, grab your coats and come with me," says Rock.

"Awww, man, it's cold!" Antwan groans.

"That's why you grab your coat," Rock tells him. "Let's ride."

We walk out to Rock's truck, and right away, I have a feeling I know where he's taking us. We ride to the other side of town with the heat and Rock's oldie music blasting.

"Yo, turn it down!" Antwan's sitting up front and tries to hide under the hood of his coat. Doesn't work. Rock actually turns the music up even more, and sings along, too! I'm not gonna say this out loud, but it's a good thing Rock's a barber not a singer!

We turn into Oakwood Plaza, which is in an area that the city is trying to build up. It's not in the best shape right now, though, and I can't help but frown a little. The building is *not* what I expected. Looks like Rock will have a lot of fixing up to do.

"We going inside?" Antwan asks, already taking his seat belt off.

"Nah, not yet," Rock says. He's got this smile on his face, and he's watching the place like it's his baby or something.

"Know what hard work is, gentlemen? It's waking up early to fix up one shop, working all day in the other shop, only to come back and work on the first one some more!"

"I could be helping, you know," Antwan grumbles. Me and him both volunteered to help get the new shop ready, but Rock always tells us no.

"With some dreams, you gotta put in the work and sweat all by yourself," Rock says. "Makes it mean more. But don't y'all worry; I got plans for both of you!"

Rock turns around to look at me.

"Isaiah, you got a poem ready for the new spot?"

"Yeah, it's already in my notebook," I say.

"Right on," Rock says with a wink.

"You mean, *write* on," I say, pretending to write in the air.

"Corn!" Antwan makes a face and shakes his head. Me and Rock laugh.

"Li'l man, there's no wrong to your write!" Rock says.

"I think you're write!" I add.

Antwan groans and says he'd rather have the music than me and Rock's corny jokes. But we don't stop. We go back and forth the rest of the drive, and it just feels . . . write.

December 12

Mama's school finished before ours, so she takes me and Charlie to the movies to celebrate . . . on a school night!

"Mama, you sure?" I ask for the second time as we drive to the theater.

"Yes, Isaiah, I'm sure!" Mama laughs. "It's not a late show, so we'll be back in plenty of time for bed."

"Can we do this again when me and Charlie are done?" I ask.

"Sure! Celebrating is important, and we're gonna do more of that."

"Yay!" Charlie cheers. She presses her face to her window and points. "Look, 'Saiah, she has a dog!"

"Yes, and she's walking it in the freezing cold," Mama says.

"It's not that cold," I say.

"I would walk Superdog even in the snow!" Charlie adds.

"Mmmmhmmm," Mama says.

We share a bucket of popcorn at the movies, and it's probably the best popcorn I've ever had. The movie we watch is pretty funny, and me and Charlie nudge Mama every time a dog comes on screen, which is a lot.

"Well, it looks like I picked the wrong movie!" Mama says after, like, the seventh nudge. I think we're getting to her.

After the movie, we sit in the theater while the credits roll, which is a Dunn family tradition. We're always the last ones to leave, cuz we have this game where everyone tries to find their name in the credits and the first one to spot it gets an extra snack on the way out. Usually, Charlie's the one who wins, but today it's Mama. When I look over to tell her I see her name, I see something I haven't seen in a while. Sadness.

"Mama, you okay?" I ask, hating the squeaky way my voice sounds.

Mama takes a deep breath and grabs me and Charlie's hands.

"You two are growing so fast!" she says. "It just hit me that one day, you'll be going to movies with your friends instead."

"No, we won't, Mama," Charlie says. "You can come, too!"

Mama does one of those happy/sad smiles and chuckles, dabbing her eyes with a napkin.

"You say that now, Charlie, but notice how quiet your big brother is!" Mama nudges me until I can't help but smile. "See!"

"Nah, Mama, it's not like that!" I say. "I'll go to the movies with you guys sometimes, and with my friends sometimes."

"I know, baby, and that's exactly what it's supposed to be," Mama says.

"It's the circle of life," I say, which makes Mama laugh.

"Well, I guess there's only one thing left for us to do," Mama says.

"What?" asks Charlie.

"Go get my snack!" Mama says, tickling Charlie till she squeals.

And even though it was only Mama who saw her name on the screen, she gets each of us an extra snack, too.

December 18

"Does GOOL have real magic?"

The Rockets Reach Back kids are making gift baskets to give away, and me and Kobe are at the Kraft Macaroni & Cheese station. Each basket gets two boxes, but Kobe hands me three when he asks his question.

"Yeah, that's what gave Kobe's basketball special powers," I say. I hold out the extra box, but he shakes his head.

"Nah, give that basket some extra cheesy magic," he says. A few minutes later, he asks another question.

"You think there's a place like GOOL in real life? It's a graveyard, right?"

"Yeah," I say with a shrug. "But it's the biggest graveyard in the city, you know, like Riverside Gardens. That's where my dad is buried."

"Really?" Kobe says. "Can I go there?"

"Only if you had a magic basketball with you," I say. "Plus, I bet you would be too scared to go."

"Me? Nah, I would walk in there just like this!"

Kobe sticks his chest out and walks like he's the tallest guy around. It's pretty funny!

"What would you do with the magic?" I ask. For once, Kobe doesn't have anything to say. He just shrugs and hands me the next two boxes of macaroni. When he stays quiet for a while, though, I start to wonder if he's okay.

"You aight?" I ask.

"Yeah," he says. "I'm tired of these baskets, though. Ready to go shoot on the real ones!"

Not gonna lie, I am, too. But by the time we finish and help load the baskets onto Ms. Marlee's truck, it's time for us to go home. Kobe dribbles while we wait for our rides, but he's still quiet.

"When's your dad get back?" I ask. "He'll get to catch some of your games, right?"

"Soon. Probably next week," Kobe says. "I think his team is playing in a championship or something right now."

"Cool!" I say. "Maybe I can get his autograph."

"He doesn't really do that," Kobe says, "but I'll see. There's my granny. See you later."

A blast of cold air hits me when Kobe opens the door and

walks outside, and I bet his hands are freezing since he never wears gloves. When Mama picks me up, I ask her if we can stop at SportsCave, which is where Sneaky gets all his football stuff.

"You got SportsCave money?" Mama asks. Man, that's gotta be her favorite thing to say! Truth is, most of my money has been going to the *Bucket Chronicles,* but I made sure to save some for Christmas gifts.

"Yes, Mama," I groan. "I wanna get Kobe a gift."

"Awww, that's sweet of you," Mama says with a smile. Got her!

It doesn't take me long to find a nice pair of gloves for Kobe, the kind with little grippers on them so he can still play ball. When we're back in the car, I shoot my shot with one more question.

"Mama, can we stop by the pet store? I wanna get Charlie a Christmas present, too."

Mama laughs and shakes her head.

"Nice try, Isaiah. But we are *not* getting a dog!"

I watch Mama's face when she says it, and she doesn't seem *absolutely* sure.

December 20

"You guys going to Atlanta for Christmas?"

It's the last day of school before break, and that means a special holiday lunch, which Sneaky is shoveling in his mouth like it's the best thing ever.

"Nope, we'll be here," Angel says. At least she's eating her food like a normal person.

"Oh wow, shocking!" Sneaky says, his mouth full of mashed potatoes.

"Whatever," Angel says, rolling her eyes. "Are *you* going away, Sneaky?"

"Nope!"

"Too bad." Angel shakes her head. "We could all use the break!"

"Whatever," Sneaky says. "Y'all would miss me."

"Maybe Aliya, but that's it!" Angel says, cracking up. I crack up, too, and almost spit out my milk! Sneaky can't even say anything, either, cuz everybody knows he likes Aliya. And it's almost like she hears us talking, cuz she appears out of nowhere and sets her tray down next to Sneaky's.

"Hey," she says, smiling at him all nice. When she sees our faces, she goes, "What? What happened?"

Me and Angel laugh some more. Maybe it won't be long until me, her, and Sneaky are all laughing together.

The rest of the day goes by super slow, probably because we're all tired of Christmas crossword puzzles and we just wanna be done with school. In my last hour of the day, language arts, there's an announcement and a lot of kids are called down to the library.

"Yo, you got in trouble the day before break?" asks Sneaky after we hear my name.

"No," I say. "It's gotta be for Rockets Reach Back cuz they called Angel, too."

When I get to the library, I see Angel, Tayshaun, Harmoni, and all the other mentors.

"I bet we about to get something," Angel says when she sees Ms. Marlee standing at a table with a giant box.

"What you think it is?" I ask.

"I dunno." Angel shrugs. "Probably some books or pencils and stuff. You know the kinda stuff teachers be giving."

The good thing is, Angel's wrong. After Ms. Marlee thanks us for being in the program and tells us we've been doing such a great job, she hands us each a gift bag.

"This is just a small token of my appreciation for each of you," Ms. Marlee says.

We all tear into the bags right away. There's a rocket-shaped stress ball, two tickets to the children's museum, red and green Hershey's kisses, a McDonald's gift card, and an ornament with a group picture of all of us.

"Awww, Ms. Marlee, you so sweet!" Angel says, grinning. "There's actually some nice stuff in here; I'm gonna have to hide it from my brothers!"

I'll probably have to do the same thing with Charlie because she snuck so much of my Halloween candy, we were still finding wrappers weeks later!

When I get home, I dump everything out to find hiding places. That's when I see that Ms. Marlee also wrote something on a Christmas tree sticky note. It says, *Merry Christmas, Isaiah! Keep changing lives, one word at a time!* I hang the ornament on our tree and put the note on the inside cover of my gold notebook. Since I'm feeling pretty inspired, I start writing the next *Bucket Chronicles,* Christmas edition.

December 25, Part 1

"Look, 'Saiah, it's Superdog! Look! Look!"

We just finished opening presents, and now Charlie's screaming her head off from the living room window. When I get over there, she's got her face smashed against it, tapping hard and yelling, "Come here, puppy!"

"Charlie, quit banging on the window!" I tell her, walking closer to see. She's right; there's a dog out there and it's walking down the sidewalk. Charlie ignores me about the window and taps some more, but the dog keeps going, tail wagging and all.

"It's Superdog, and he's cold!" Charlie says.

"That ain't Superdog, Charlie," I say. "Probably just somebody's lost pet."

"Oh, that's sad," she says softly. "It's Christmas!"

"Dogs don't celebrate Christmas, Charlie," I say.

"You don't know that!" Charlie replies. "They celebrate

everything we do, only better, and I think Superdog wants to come inside."

I shake my head and pat Mama's arm.

"Toldja we shoulda got Charlie a dog for Christmas," I say. "That would keep her busy alllll day, like the sister she never had!"

"Yeah, Mama, I want a sister, too!" Charlie says.

"I think it's time to talk about something else," Mama says. "Like who's gonna help me wash the greens for dinner!"

"Not me!" I say quickly. I helped Mama with that before, and it took *forever*!

Lucky for me, there's a knock on the door, and I walk to the hall closet to grab my coat, hat, and gloves before I open it and let Sneaky in.

" 'Saiah, are you gonna go get Superdog?" Charlie squeals.

"You still on Superdog, Charlie?" says Sneaky, stepping inside.

"He's outside, Sneaky, look!" Charlie drags Sneaky to the window so he can see. The dog is wandering back down the street now.

"Yo, Superdog's mad small!" Sneaky says.

"That's why nobody thinks he has powers," Charlie tells him. "But he does!"

"Nice," Sneaky says, patting Charlie's shoulder, then turning to me. "You ready, bro?"

"Yup, just gotta get my backpack," I say.

Kobe only lives a couple of blocks away, and Mama said Sneaky and I could walk over to give him his gift. Sneaky's tagging along cuz he's got a gift, too . . . for Aliya! He was too chicken to give it to her at school, but she lives on the same street as Kobe.

"Where are you going?" asks Charlie.

"We'll be right back," I tell her. "We gotta deliver some gifts."

"Yeah, we out here like Santa," Sneaky says.

"Y'all be quick and come right back. Miz Rita's gonna be making Christmas cookies for us to decorate," says Mama.

Sneaky snickers and whispers, "Lame!" and I elbow him. Decorating cookies might be wack to him, but it's way better than what we did last Christmas, which was sit in our apartment in the dark—no Christmas tree or lights—eating peanut butter and crackers for dinner.

" 'Saiah, I have a present for Superdog so I need to come, too," Charlie says.

"No, baby, you're gonna stay here and help me with these greens, remember?" Mama says.

Charlie sighs all loud but says, "Ooo-kay."

"It's, like, the perfect Christmas," Sneaky says when we get outside. Snowflakes are swirling and it's not too cold, so yeah, it feels perfect.

"You think she's gonna like the present?" I ask.

"Man, she better!" Sneaky says. "This stuff was over twenty bucks!"

Sneaky got Aliya a perfume thing and some lotion, said his mom helped him pick it out. The gift is in a fancy red bag with tissue paper and everything! Probably his mom's idea. I wrapped my gifts for Kobe, but I put them in my backpack to carry them. Now I'm wishing I had a bag like Sneaky's.

We split up when we get to Kobe and Aliya's block, so I don't have to see how pathetically mushy Sneaky is when he gives Aliya her gift. Kobe's grandma answers the door with a loud, "Who is it?" but the second she sees it's me, a huge smile covers her face.

"Well, merry Christmas, Mr. Lifesaver!" she says with a wink. "How ya doing?"

"Merry Christmas," I say. "I'm good, just dropping off Kobe's present."

"That's so sweet of you!" his grandma says. She calls for Kobe a few times, then tells me to go on back to his room.

"He probably on that game machine," she says, shaking her head.

I go down the hall to his room, and even though the TV is on, no one's in there. I call him a few times, check his messy closet, and then come back out.

"Ummm, Kobe's not in there," I say. "Do you want me to just leave the gift?"

"Not in there?" Kobe's grandma scrunches up her face, and

she calls again. When Kobe doesn't answer, she walks down the hall to check for herself. There's a frown on her face when she comes back.

"Well, his brand-new basketball is gone, so he's probably out at some playground. I told that boy a thousand times to stop sneaking out to play!"

"I think I know which court he's at," I tell Kobe's grandma. "I'll go get him for you."

On my way outside, I notice that there's just a small Christmas tree in the living room, and there isn't wrapping paper all over the floor, like at Miz Rita's place. I wonder if Kobe only got a few presents this year, and if his dad made it back in time.

Sneaky's coming down the street when I leave Kobe's house, and he's cheesin' hard. Guess Aliya liked her gift.

"Yo, look what she got me!" Sneaky says, holding up an Axe body spray set.

"Yeah, she knows you stink!" I say. Sneaky punches me on the shoulder.

"I bet her mom helped her with this, too," he says. "Moms all think the same."

"Pretty much!"

"Yo, where you going?" Sneaky asks when I walk left at the stop sign instead of right.

"Kobe wasn't there," I say. "His grandma thinks he's at the playground, so I'm gonna go get him."

Sneaky sucks his teeth and rubs his hands together.

"He out playing in the cold? On Christmas?"

"He's dedicated," I say.

"Well, let's hurry up; I'm ready for one of Miz Rita's cookies and some hot chocolate!"

"Oh, so now you wanna make cookies?" I say.

"I didn't say make 'em." Sneaky laughs. "I said eat 'em!"

Sneaky opens the box as we walk and sprays the cologne on me, then at the snowflakes that are falling faster. We both smell like Ice Chill and Cool Ocean by the time we get to the playground . . . the *empty* playground.

"Man, he ain't even here!" Sneaky groans.

"C'mon, let's check the one by the library," I say. "That's like his favorite court."

"It's also like ten minutes away, bro," Sneaky says.

"So we'll be fast," I say, starting to run. "Pretend it's for football!"

"Yo! Slow down!"

For once, it's Sneaky huffing and puffing behind me. We walk/jog to the library, and I'm breathing hard by the time we go around to the court.

"Brooo!" Sneaky groans again, leaning over to catch his breath.

I'm out of breath, too, but I don't stop to think about it cuz one look around the court tells me everything I need to know.

Kobe's not here, either.

December 25, Part 2

"He probably went home, 'Saiah," Sneaky says, bouncing from one foot to the other.

We race over to Kobe's place, and I'm not gonna lie, my teeth are chattering by the time we get there. The karate-chopping starts in my stomach when Kobe's grandma opens the door and he's not at home. I'm starting to feel the same way I did when Charlie wandered off on her birthday.

"That boy's gonna be in a heap of trouble!" Kobe's grandma says, but I can tell she's getting worried. "I better drive around and look for him. Do you boys need a ride home?"

"Yes, please," Sneaky says at the same time I say, "No thanks."

Sneaky's eyes bug out as he stares at me.

"It's no trouble. I can drop you home. Let me just get my purse."

"We need to check a few more parks," I whisper to Sneaky when she leaves the room.

"Bro, my mom is texting me a million times! Your mom must've told her we're not back," Sneaky whispers.

Yikes! It's never a pretty picture when our moms get mad at us together. When they double-teamed us last summer, we got grounded for a week—no TV, no video games, no selling candy. All we did was clean everything in sight!

Kobe's grandma tells me I can leave the gifts in Kobe's room.

Sneaky comes with me, and I put everything on his bed. Gloves, a book about Kobe Bryant, and a basketball stress ball (got that idea from Ms. Marlee). The best gift, though, is my Christmas edition of the *Bucket Chronicles.*

"Yo, check it out; he was reading my books!" I tell Sneaky, noticing a few *Bucket Chronicles* on Kobe's bed.

"Musta been bored and couldn't sleep," Sneaky jokes. I punch him on the shoulder and pick up the first book, which is opened to the page where superhero Kobe goes to GOOL for the first time. There's some scribbles on the next page, but Sneaky nudges me and says we gotta go.

On the quick ride home, we're all staring out the windows, hoping we see Kobe walking. No luck.

"Did Kobe's dad make it back from overseas?" I ask. "Maybe he took him to an inside gym to play."

"Overseas?" Kobe's grandma frowns as she looks at me in the rearview mirror. "His father isn't overseas. Who told you that?"

"Kobe did." I gulp. "He said his dad played basketball overseas but was coming home for Christmas."

"Oh my word! Seems like my grandson got some of your storytelling abilities," Kobe's grandma says. She sighs. "Kobe's dad has been real sick for the past year, in and out of the hospital. He's getting better, but he still has to have treatments. His mom is there now, and we're supposed to visit him later today. I don't see why that boy took off like this!"

"You think he ran away?" asks Sneaky.

"I don't know what I think," she says.

Me and Sneaky are real quiet after that, and when we get to our building, I take out my notebook and write down my mom's number, Miz Rita's number, *and* Sneaky's number.

"Can you please call us when you find him?" I ask, handing Kobe's grandma the piece of paper.

"I surely will," she says. "Thank you for your help."

"Yo, did you know that about his dad?" Sneaky asks as we walk inside.

"Nah," I say. Ms. Marlee was right; there's a lot of Kobe's story that I don't know.

Both our moms are waiting for us at Miz Rita's house, arms folded and storm-cloud faces. Sneaky talks fast.

"Whoa, before y'all get angry, 'Saiah's little brother guy is missing, and we were trying to find him."

"What?" says Mama.

"Kobe's grandma doesn't know where he is," I say. "Me and Sneaky were checking the basketball courts where he plays."

"Oh no!" Mama says. "Is there anything we can do to help?"

"I don't know." I shrug. "I gave her your number to call."

"You have any idea where he might be?" Miz Rita asks.

"No," I say. Other than playgrounds, I don't know where Kobe would go, especially on Christmas, when he's supposed to visit his dad.

"Well, make sure you think about it," Mama says. "Something might come to you. Hopefully we'll get a call soon."

"We started the cookies without you, but you can still make some," Charlie says.

"No thanks," I say. "We're just gonna hang out in my room."

"Man, my fingers are frozen!" Sneaky says, flopping on my bed.

"Should've worn gloves," I say, which makes me think about the gift I got Kobe. The gift he would've had right now if he had been home.

I sit down and grab my notebook, but I don't feel any words coming. If they did come, they'd all be sad. So instead, I pull out the basket from under my bed and grab a different notebook, one that has words already there.

"Whatchoo doing?" Sneaky asks.

"Reading," I say. It's not as weird as saying, "I'm asking Daddy for help, in the only way I can."

I flip through the first notebook, looking for anything Daddy might've written about lost kids on Christmas. Nothing. I do the same with the second notebook. It's more of a journal with his feelings and stuff. Even though I don't find any answers, I feel better after reading.

Sneaky's phone starts ringing, and his eyes bug out when he looks at it.

"What? Is it his grandma?" I ask.

Sneaky shakes his head.

"Nah, it's Angel," he says. "It's a video call."

Angel? What she calling for? When Sneaky answers, Angel's face fills the screen and I can hear her across the room.

"Are you still with Isaiah? Did you guys find him?"

"Yo, how does she even know?" I whisper.

"I put something on Snapchat while we were running," Sneaky whispers back.

"Angel follows you on Snap?"

"HELLO?? You know I can hear you guys, right?"

Angel rolls her eyes on the screen, and Sneaky shakes his head and hands the phone to me.

"'Saiah, what happened?"

"I don't know," I say. "I think he ran away."

"That's not good," Angel says. She starts firing questions and I tell her what I know, even the stuff about his dad.

"So his basketball was the only thing missing?" Angel asks.

"Yeah, but he wasn't at any of the courts we checked," I say.

"Maybe there's another court he goes to," Angel suggests. "Where else would he go with the ball?"

I tell Angel I don't know, but I'm thinking hard enough to make my brain explode.

"Maybe it'll help if you write things down," Angel suggests.

So I do. I grab my notebook and write down everything I know:

1. Kobe got a new ball for Christmas.
2. Maybe he went outside to play with it?
3. He's not at any of the courts around here . . . did he get lost?
4. Kobe was reading *Bucket Chronicles* Part 1.
5. Kobe's dad isn't overseas, but he *is* sick.
6. Kobe's supposed to visit his dad today, so why would he leave?

"Maybe he's going to get his dad a present," Sneaky says, reading over my shoulder.

"Yeah, but why would he take the ball with him?" I ask.

"Maybe he thinks it's magic," Angel says. "Like in the story."

My stomach starts karate-chopping, but not because I'm nervous. I think about how Kobe asked if GOOL was real, and how he might be thinking his dad needs a little magic today. When all those things come together, there's only one place he could be.

"Yo, guys, I know where he is!"

December 25, Part 3

CLUES

Time's running out;
I don't know what to do.
They're counting on me,
But I can't find the clue!
I don't have any answers,
Don't know where to look.
I checked in the safe,
In the box,
In the book.
I listened to messages,
I read every text.
My brain's going wild;
What should I check next?
To the kitchen I go
For one giant bowl.
Beans and rice,
Hot and nice,
Now I'm ready to roll!
Superhero I am,
Superhero is me,
I'm finding the clues
For everybody.

The bus ride is bumpy, but I manage to finish my poem. I put my notebook in my backpack and stare out the window as the city zooms by.

"We're gonna be in so much trouble," Sneaky says for the third time.

"Not if we find him," I say.

"I don't know, bro," Sneaky says. "You really think he went to some made-up place to get some magic that ain't real?"

When Sneaky says it out loud, it does sound kinda weird. But it's my only idea. It feels just like a movie, how the main character has to remember something from a long time ago to solve a mystery right now. Superhero Isaiah Dunn had to do that in one of Daddy's stories, and I'm doing it now. I just hope I'm right.

"Can't believe I'm saying this," Angel says with a groan, "but Sneaky might be right, for the first time ever."

"Maaannn!" goes Sneaky.

"Guys, chill; we're almost there," I say.

I never thought it could happen, but me and my two business partners are *finally* working together. Angel grabbed one of those bus route brochures so we could figure out where we're going and met us at the bus stop on Creighton, a street we're definitely *not* supposed to go on. Me and Sneaky told our moms and Miz Rita that we knew where Kobe might be, and we dashed out the door before they could ask any questions. Judging by how many calls Sneaky's getting, they're not really feelin' our plan. But it's too late to turn back now!

The bus stops right where Angel said it would, a block away from Riverside Gardens, the place where Daddy is buried.

"You good?" Sneaky asks me as we hurry to the entrance.

"Yeah," I say. I think Mama has come here a few times, but not me. Once was enough.

"Okay, where you think he might be?" Angel asks. "What did you write in the story?"

"'The Garden of Orange Legends' was all made up," I say. "Kobe found the basketball in an area with a pond and an orange bench."

"Ummm, I don't think none of that is here," Angel says, looking around.

"Let's go this way," I say, taking a path to the left.

"Can't believe I'm in a cemetery on Christmas," Sneaky mutters, following us.

We walk for a few minutes, and I'm starting to think this was a bad idea. But then I hear something.

Thump! Thump! Thump!

"Hey, did y'all hear that?" I ask. Everyone freezes and listens.

"Yo, this is like that movie where they get trapped in the story," Sneaky says, eyes wide.

"Stop being scary!" Angel says. "That's a ball bouncing!"

We start yelling for Kobe and run toward the thumping sound.

"Look! I think that's him!" Angel yells when we see someone on a bench up ahead.

"Isaiah? What you doing here?" Kobe asks when we reach him.

"Me? What are *you* doing here?" I ask. "Your grandma and everybody is worried about you!"

"Why? I left her a note," Kobe says, his face all scrunched up.

"Bro, we were in your room. We didn't see any note," Sneaky says.

"It's in the *Chronicles* Part 1, but it was a secret code. I thought she would get it," Kobe says. "Is my granny here, too?"

"No, just us," I say, sitting down beside him. "Your grandma told me about your dad. Is that why you came here?"

Kobe stares at his shoes and nods.

"If all that stuff you wrote was real, it could make him better, right?" he asks, his voice sounding small.

"Maybe," I say. "But I think I know what's already making him better."

"I know," Kobe sighs. "Them doctors and the medicine."

"Nah, man, *you*!" I say. "That's why we gotta get you back home."

"About that," Sneaky says, looking at his phone. "I kinda had to tell my mom where we are, sooo they're on the way. Probably won't be pretty."

"You sure there ain't no magic in this ball?" I ask, dribbling a few times. "I think we're gonna need it."

Kobe steals the ball back and grins.

"You already know!" he says, sounding more like himself. "Nothin' but magic when I got the ball!"

December 31

Last day of the year, and we're out the house for the first time since Christmas, celebrating the grand opening of New Growth #2. Mama said we're not gonna stay long, but it's already been an hour and everyone is having fun, especially me and Sneaky. It sucks to be grounded over Christmas break, but hey, it was for a good reason!

Rock's second barbershop looks AMAZING inside! I guess he really did have a vision. He says New Growth #1 is Old School and New Growth #2 is New School, his dream for the young barbers coming up. I really think he means Antwan when he says that.

Rock has flat-screen TVs everywhere, and even a PS5 for people to play while they wait for a cut. His barber chairs are fancy, too—red and black and super comfy. Music's playing, and not his old-people music, either; it's music that's actually out right now! My favorite part of the shop, though, is the poster-size version of the poem I wrote for Rock. He made my words really big and put my name at the bottom so everyone will know who wrote it. Mama likes that part, too.

Lots of people are here for the opening/New Year's party, and Mrs. Rock warns me, Sneaky, and Antwan that we're gonna miss out on the food if we keep playing video games. We take a break and pile our plates with wings and cheese and crackers. Sneaky's mom makes us put baby carrots and broccoli on our plates, too. Moms be doing the most!

"So, Mr. Rock, whatchoo think about my idea? It's New School, right?" Sneaky says. He's been trying to convince Rock to let him sell the Candy Boy Shake out of the barbershop.

"Get your recipe right, and bring me and the missus some samples we can't resist," Rock says, patting Sneaky on the back. "Then we'll talk."

"Aight, bet!" Sneaky says, and he looks like one of those cartoon characters when they get dollar signs in their eyes.

Charlie's been running around with the stuffed dog I got her for Christmas, but I know she doesn't like him as much as the REAL dog we got a few days ago! Technically, Miz Rita got him, but we all know she did it for Charlie. We couldn't believe that little dog from Christmas kept coming around. Miz Rita didn't want to see him in the cold, so she said we're holding on to him until somebody claims him. So far, nobody has, even after we put up signs, made posts all over social media, and took him to see a vet. To be honest, the dog fits in perfectly with everybody, like he's supposed to be with us. He's the color of honey, and the vet said he's a goldendoodle, which is a mix between a golden retriever and a poodle. And no matter what Charlie does to him, his tail stays wagging!

"He sho' is growing on me!" Miz Rita says, patting him on the head.

"He's a cute li'l guy," Rock says. "What's his name, Charlie?"

"'Saiah's gonna pick his name," Charlie says.

Huh?

"I thought you named him Superdog," I say.

"This is Superdog," she tells me, holding up the stuffed dog. "You get to name the real one."

"What's it gonna be, li'l man?" Rock asks. "He gotta have a name before the New Year."

I think about everything that's happened this year, good things and not-so-good things. I think about Mama and me and Charlie being safe and much happier. I think about Miz Rita and Rock and Mr. Shephard and Kobe, about Sneaky and Angel and how they talk without arguing now. (Well, not really, but I bet they will soon!) I think about Daddy, and how he'll always be with us. When all those thoughts mix together in my mind, I come up with the perfect name for our dog.

"Hero," I say. "His name's gonna be Hero."

And I think the sky must agree with me, because it explodes into early fireworks, almost like it's saying, *Welcome home, Hero.*

ACKNOWLEDGMENTS

When I first wrote "The Beans and Rice Chronicles of Isaiah Dunn," I had no idea that this Isaiah kid would have so much to say! The more I listened, the more I discovered that his words and thoughts echo those of countless kids who are experiencing loss, grief, joy, creativity, and the desire to be a solid pillar for someone else.

I also had no idea that I'd be going through loss myself while writing this, or that I could grieve so much for someone I've never met. I want to acknowledge those whose support and understanding during this time have been invaluable.

My parents: Not only have you kept, fed, and transported

my kids, done laundry, washed dishes, and cleaned bathrooms, but you also served as virtual educators for a whole school year! Eternal thanks!

My kids: You will forever be forced to watch/listen to Kobe videos, interviews, games, and personal repetition from me. Most of you have embraced it. Trust me; it's easier if you do. ☺

My sisters, Kim and Karmen: You guys have driven me so I could ride and write more times than I can count, and that little thing means so much! I love you both!

My bro-in-law, Pierre: You're probably the only one I personally know who loves Kobe as much as I do. Thank you for being there on the tough days and for always having a video to share!

I grew up hangin' with the guys all the time, but now I am blessed with an infantry of powerful women who keep me lifted up: Jayne, Afiya, Jordan, Sherina, Trish, Brenda, Sue, Mary, Liz, Dillondria, Mrs. Saleeby, and Bella! Thank you for your love and support!

To Phoebe, Elizabeth, and my Crown family, your PATIENCE and support have been incredible. Thank you for both pushing me and giving me space to create!

To Hannah, this was a year full of celebrations, and I'm glad we got to experience so many of them together!

One of my favorite Kobe quotes is on the wall in my room:

"The most important thing is to try and inspire people so that they can be great in whatever they want to do." Your impact on others will outlive you, so go forth and SAVE THE DAY, in your own way!

ABOUT THE AUTHOR

Kelly J. Baptist is the inaugural winner of the We Need Diverse Books short-story contest. Her story is featured in the WNDB anthology *Flying Lessons & Other Stories* and inspired her first full-length novel, *Isaiah Dunn Is My Hero*. Kelly was surprised when Isaiah kept talking to her, but by now she knows to listen. *Isaiah Dunn Saves the Day* came from her desire to show the bravery, kindness, and indomitable spirit in every kid. That's why *they* are her heroes. Every day.

Kelly is also the author of the picture book *The Electric Slide and Kai* and the middle-grade novel *The Swag Is in the Socks*. Kelly works as a middle-school Social Emotional Learning Interventionist and lives in southwest Michigan with her five amazing children. You can learn more about Kelly on her website kellyiswrite.com.

Ready for your next great Kelly J. Baptist read?
Soar into a story now!

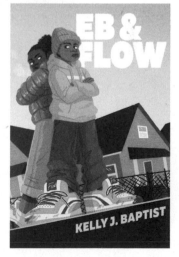